THE GRE

DIARIES

DAY 1 - 100

BY PATRICK W. MARSH

Cover Designed by Geneva Lerwick

Special Acknowledgements

Troy Nellis, Brian Baumgart, and Karen Evans at NHCC for their continued support,

My father, mother, and sister, even though they're slightly terrified to read my work,

And for Geneva,

Who taught me what it's liked to be loved

The following collections of journals were recovered from a caravan outside of Duluth, Minnesota. The exact date of recovery is not known nor is the origin of the speaker. The Bureau for the Restoration of History (BFRH) would like help in identifying the man who kept these records. This unedited record of events is still considered the most accurate history of the apocalypse that occurred on April 15th, 2011.

THE DRUM

Day One

I took a yellow memo pad from the supply locker. I hope they don't care. I need to write something down. I remember hearing somewhere that having a journal is a good way to avoid going crazy. It was on the Today Show or something like that. They'd have to be experts, right? Doesn't matter, I won't get in trouble. The bank won't be working for a while. I don't care though, after everything that's happened. I don't want to work here anymore if this is going to happen in the area.

It hit around six tonight—right before I could close the drive up.

There was this weird hammering sound everywhere. I thought it was just some construction, but it didn't stop. It started, and the drumming came through every wall and counter. It was almost like a casual vibration or something.

They came shortly after, the screams.

At first they were everywhere around the building, people screaming, running, and being chased. A fat, white guy with a Twins jersey on came running by the bank's windows and something grabbed him from underneath the window. There was a scream, crunch, and nothing else. I hid down behind the counters. Something exploded outside, sending a tree branch into the front doors, throwing glass everywhere. I crawled to the basement.

There were more explosions, like they were following me. The lights went out quickly and without warning. I heard some brakes screech and a woman screaming. The door to the basement still worked, a battery controlled the whole thing. Three hours since then, my phone is holding the time at least. I'm going to hide here all night. The mold and dust smell is driving me a little nuts. The basement had a few cookies, and stale chips from the office parties. I ate them all. I don't care. I tried calling my Dad, Sister, and my girlfriend. No answer, nothing, not a whisper. It was probably like 9/11 when the phones crashed or when Michael Jackson died. I'm going to try and sleep soon. The walls keep shaking, and there are distant sounds of smashes and screams.

War? The Russians? An earthquake in Saint Paul? Whatever, I'm not going to sit down here all night. I'll have to pee eventually. The bathroom is upstairs. I'll try and sleep first, and I see if I can drive home in the morning. My dog is home after all. She hates thunderstorms.

She can't be doing very well with this.

Day Two

They came back. I had hoped they wouldn't, but they're here. The sound started again just a few moments ago. Most people left their cars. I didn't. I crawled into the trunk through my seats. I'm not going out there. I've got some old Taco Bell back here that smells funky and some empty quarts of oil that made the carpet greasy. Should've listened to my girlfriend and thrown them away. I hear all sorts of things around me, screams, explosions, and the grating sound of shattered glass being walked on. I never should have left the bank.

When I woke up this morning, the world was hot and humid. I could feel the heat bubbling down into that dank basement. It's April? It shouldn't be this hot. I made it outside and found everything smashed; cars turned over and charred. A bus was torn open and was stained a deep red.

Everything smelled burnt and ugly.

A few light poles had fallen down in the bank parking lot, but both missed my Stratus. A cop had started to wave traffic through the street; a bulldozer was pushing all the shit out of the way. Houses were smashed; their roofs taken off and walls torn out. The plants were budding like crazy. And the heat, the damn heat was everywhere. I asked the police officer what happened and he said, "We got attacked by some sort of thing last night, devils or something. I'd try and make it home. They seemed to have gone away in the daylight. A bunch of people died though. Prepare yourself. I don't know much more than that, but everyone is trying to get home."

He looked at the bank behind me and shook his head.

"Well, money isn't that important now, huh?" he said.

That wasn't my money, so whatever.

I jumped in my car and turned on the radio. There was nothing. Just that annoying broadcast that they test at the beginning of the month. I-94 was getting cleared of debris and people were piling into their cars. It took me all day to get to Minneapolis. Nothing moved. My phone is dead. I got to Broadway when the sound started. There is nothing else. I have to stop writing. I've never written this much in my life. Things are walking by my car.

I can feel their weight.

Day Three

I heard all the carnage from my trunk. The night happened and that sound drummed. It was an endless collection of screams and explosions. When I got out in the morning, almost all the cars were empty around me. They were all either turned over, smashed, or burning a slow stench of oily fire.

I smelled something cooking; it could have been skin. I wanted to vomit, but I was empty.

People had looted liquor stores, stolen electronics, and broken into fast food restaurants. There were some cops around, but they were covered in blood and dirt. They didn't look real cognitive as they were being bombarded by a frantic horde of screaming people asking them about their loved ones. An old guy walked up to me and told me that we'd been attacked again. Nobody knew by what or how, but they were dispatching National Guard troops to the worse areas. He said it happened everywhere and that the things attacking were insane, but I already knew that.

It took me six hours to walk home.

My dog is still alive. She's a Miniature Dachshund. She was out of water, food, and went all over the floor. I had to clean it up right away. A big maple tree had fallen on my house. Luckily, my house is so tiny that the tree branches basically tangled it, instead of smashing right through it. It gives the destroyed appearance pretty well I'd say. No one else has been to my house. Not my girlfriend and not my family. The door was still locked. None of the windows were broken. The power is down, which makes sense.

15

There are literally hundreds of live power-lines dancing around everywhere. There are a few power crews out trying to contain them, and by few, I mean two.

I ate some cheese and meat before it spoiled. At least I'll lose weight like my family and girlfriend wanted. I've got a gun too; a 22 gauge shotgun with a box of shells. I used it for duck hunting once a year.

I'm going to sleep in the basement tonight with my dog. I hope she doesn't bark. She seems exhausted, so it should be okay. I've got a wrist watch, so I can pay attention to when that drumming starts again. I know it'll start.

I know it.

Day Four

Last night passed slowly. The drum started at exactly 8:37 p.m. It had started earlier the past two days. We didn't move the entire night. I slept underneath the stairs, away from the windows. I had as many blankets as possible. My dog Snowy had insomnia when I was gone, so she slept soundly underneath my arm the entire night. The basement was cold and musky. I hid my sneezes the best I could. Between the drumming was an eerie silence. People must've been prepared. I wanted to light a candle and look at a few pictures of my family and girlfriend, but it seemed like every time I moved, something scratched against the outside of the house. Occasionally, something walked by and made dust fall from the ceiling. Closer to dawn, there were a few screams.

They made me cry, and that made me sleep.

I took a cold shower this afternoon. There was something strange about my reflection in the mirror besides the overweight white guy I normally would see. There was some sort of shadow behind me, like someone was looking over my shoulder. It made my skin ache. I covered the mirror with a bed sheet.

The house was sticky. The temperature was out of control. While I took my dog out, I was able to look around my neighborhood. Cars were the same as everywhere else, smashed and burnt. Trees were budding wildly, along with flowers and bushes. Ivy was growing along the road.

How were things growing so fast?

Dried spots of blood stained the grass in my front yard. I was done exploring after that. I fiddled around with my phone and eventually got a charge through my laptop, and used it to call everyone. The network was still down. I listened to everyone's voicemail. They made me feel better. I know I'll have to eventually look for everyone. I'm too scared though. I hate myself. My neighbor across the alley has boarded up his house. Every window and door was blocked by black pieces of wood. I didn't even notice him working on it.

Not many people were moving around.

I moved all the food I could into my small basement. After that, I managed to light the burner on my gas stove. Macaroni and cheese never tasted so good.

Better stop; the evening is coming to an end.

Day Five

Last night, I saw them.

They got him, my neighbor across the alley. He was the one who boarded up his house. They knew someone was in there; they knew it. I watched them from my basement window. He had a gun too; I heard it firing through the drum. I only saw them for a second. They were shadowy, long, and not completely there. They were surrounded by something. Not clothing, but a dark cloud. Some of them walked up to his house, while others crawled. A few were even on the roof. None of them looked the same shape or size. They dragged him outside. He shot a few of them with his handgun. I saw the flashes. They just looked stunned and didn't go down. They had skeletons underneath their clouds. I could see their golden outline. The big ones had claws that stretched out and stabbed him. Others had blades on their arms that smashed him over and over. He screamed for help. They tore him to pieces. It was over fast.

What are they? Are they here simply to kill us?

They knew he was in there because of the boards.

I didn't sleep last night or this morning. I couldn't. I moved more stuff to the basement, but left a few things out. If they can notice the boards on the house, what else can they notice? I thought I saw something in the door handle today. It reminded me of that shadow from yesterday. It vanished when I stared at it. There has to be a connection, you know, like in the movies.

There were more plants outside today. There are bright blue flowers growing on the ivy everywhere. I had no idea ivy even

19

bloomed flowers. I don't want to leave my house for very long. I just need to see other people around. There is nobody though. They're all too afraid to leave. At the very end of my block, there is a big oak tree with pictures stapled to it. I assume it's for missing people.

I put a blanket over the bloody stain just behind my neighbor's house. It was on the concrete. I didn't even know his name.

I'm the only one who knows he's gone.

Day Six

*Last night started quiet. There was just the drum and
nothing else. I wanted to listen to a little music. It would be worth
the battery power to drown out that endless thudding. How is there
any dust left on the ceiling? The trickle seems endless. I can't stop
thinking about my family and my girlfriend. Did they survive?
Where were they when it started? How would they have gotten away
if they'd been in the open? I'm not special, they could be living. I'm
going to have to go look for them eventually. I'll give my phone a
few more days.*

*I noticed the roof creaking heavily right before dawn. They
must've walked across it right before they vanished. The floor
groaned too, my dog whined at the sound. I know they were
upstairs. I know it.*

*In the morning, I checked my house. The door wasn't open
and none of the windows were smashed. I don't know where they
would have gotten in? I didn't move anything more to the basement.
If they had been inside, I wouldn't want them to notice anything
different. Just like my neighbor's boards. They knew about them.*

*I decided to walk a little bit further today. I brought my gun
and dog with me. The 22 was for hunting and you were only able to
keep three shots in for ducks. I took out the stopper so I could have
five. If the DNR suddenly appeared to fine me for it, well, it'd just be
nice to see them. Halfway down the block I ran into an old man
named Gerald. He lived two blocks away. He was frail, withered,
and covered in a thin layer of dirt. He carried a long rifle with a red*

21

scope. He seemed happy to see me. He said the monsters tried to get him a few nights ago. One smashed through his door when the drum started. He shot it eight times in the doorway, before it collapsed outside. He ran and hid. He said they came and got the body. Then they looked for him. He sobbed a little when he talked. He didn't even know how they found him. He had a radio too, and said the army was making a strategy to fight back.

The monsters could be killed. Everyone was hiding and waiting to come out.

This isn't the end yet. I have some hope.

Day Seven

Besides the drumming last night, it was quiet all the way through the night. It's almost more unsettling when it's just the drum. There were no scraps or bangs against the house. No screams, explosions, or strange hissing. I kept the safety off on my shotgun.

It felt good to wake up to silence.

I stacked some boxes of junk my dad had in my basement. The house used to be my grandmother's. I made a wall with his stuff. Even if they came down into the basement, the wall would look somewhat natural. My mom would be happy that his pack-ratting came in handy.

I'm impressed that the cold water is still working. The water heater isn't working; there must be something electrical with that. I've been storing water in as many containers as I can find. I figure that's practical of me. Luckily, I had just bought a whole bag of dog food before everything happened. So, at least I don't have to worry about that for a while. Food for me is going to be another story. Hopefully, when the army gets a handle on things, they'll make some sort of supply system.

It's been a week since the first night of the drum. April 17, 2011.

I should start using the date in this memo book, but that just depresses me.

I went down the street again and talked to Gerald. He gave me a cup of coffee. It tasted fantastic. He even had some cream for it. He talked about his son and daughter in Ohio and how he wanted to leave to see if they were okay. The radio was saying to stay off the roads because of debris. The army didn't have the time or people to move everything aside. They were supposed to be mounting a counter attack to lure the monsters out and bomb them. Gerald said it wouldn't work and that when the drums started, planes fell out of the sky. Since then, nobody had been flying. Gerald thought they might have something in the air, something that took all those planes down. Frightening things like people with legs and arms, but surrounded by some sort of fog. He said they had no faces and they made no sounds. Even when he shot that one in his doorway, it was silent. I talked to him all day.

The house seems a little bit lonelier tonight.

Day Eight

Last night, something happened somewhere in the neighborhood. The drum sounded at 8:14 p.m. There is no rhyme or reason to its starting time. You just know that when the sun starts to wane it could start at any moment. Around midnight, between the hollow thumps, there was a horrible crashing sound. It sounded like metal being torn. There was a terrible howling, followed by metallic pop. I don't know what it could have been. The sound was so loud that it made my teeth hurt.

It couldn't have been very far away.

In the morning, I started to look for some old maps around the house. I had to find the most efficient way to travel. I couldn't be caught in the open when the drum started, so I plotted out a path to my parent's house and my girlfriend's apartment. My parents live in the suburbs just north of Minneapolis. My girlfriend lives in Little Canada. I left my car in that roadblock on 94. I could go back to look at it. If all the highways were blocked, it wouldn't matter anyways. My dad had a spare old Jaguar. He'd had it since I was kid sitting in the backyard. It was one of many things he had difficulty parting with.

Once the army launches their counter attack, I'll start thinking about getting my car back. Until then, I'll just wait. I wish I knew when that was going to happen. Maybe they need help? I have a gun after all.

I walked down to see Gerald again today. He was waiting for me with a cup of coffee. He said a group of people had come through earlier with about a hundred wounded. They were setting up refugee camps outside the cities. I immediately went to pack, but Gerald stopped me. Gerald said he didn't trust the government to take care of him. If they didn't see these monsters coming, then why should he trust them for protection? He calmed me down and told me to stay someplace familiar until things became more stable. It's hard fighting the urge to move, but I'm doing it.

I'm worried for my dog. There are a lot of strays wandering around. How long until they get hungry? There are so many of them.

Why don't the monsters have any interest in them?

Day Nine

Last night, while the drum was beating, a shadow was standing outside one of my basement windows. The moon was full, which allowed me to notice the hulking shape. I couldn't tell whether or not it was a person or one of those things. It stood there all night. I peeked at it through a pair of uneven boxes.

My gun never left my hands. My arms are heavy from holding it all night.

In the morning when I took Snowy out, I looked at the ground next to the window. The green grass looked normal and elevated. There had been nobody there. It had to be one of those things. It felt like it was waiting for me to appear, like it was baiting me or something. When I told Gerald about it, he asked if I noticed anything about my mirrors at home. He said the night he was attacked he'd been standing in the mirror for a while. He said there was a shadow with him. He thought it was just his glaucoma and stress. He said it spread around his back. Since then he's had his mirror covered with a sheet, just like mine. Could they really be spying on us through the mirrors?

I told Gerald I had to look for my parents and girlfriend. He wished me luck.

I spent the rest of the morning getting things ready for tomorrow. I'm going to bike to my parent's house first, spend the night and then move onto my girlfriend's apartment. The air has been hot and the sky cloudless. It's been like this for nine days. I'll bring water, food, my gun, and, of course, Snowy. I can't leave her.

27

Luckily, she is a semi-small dog. Her hotdog body is a little long, so that might be tricky, but I'm going to rig up a basket of sorts on the back of my bike. I found an old white plastic crate in the basement.

What if I'm marooned and she starves to death?

I'll leave the moment the drum stops tomorrow morning. I've decided to stick to the highways that I would normally take there. My bike is narrow enough to pedal through all the debris. Later, I'll go in the shed behind my house and modify the bike.

The ivy and flowers have started to wrap up the shed as if they don't want me to open the doors.

Day Ten

The drum sounded from 9:02 pm – 5:07 am. Nothing was near my house. Nothing shook the dust free from my ceiling. Nothing scratched the roof. The moment the drum stopped I was outside. It took me about an hour to get all the vines off the shed to get my bike.

I swear the ivy and the flowers didn't want me to take it.

It took me three hours to bike to my parent's house. The freeway was clogged with broken and smashed cars. Most of them were covered with this weird ivy and blue flowers. There were bloody stains too, but grass had eaten up the highway's surface, so they were barely visible. There were people walking the opposite direction to the west, to Saint Cloud and further. There were families, senior citizens, and groups of children. Most walked, other's had bikes or motorcycles. None bothered me. They nearly blocked out the cars and the pavement. They saw I was carrying a gun. My dog use to bark at strangers, but she kept quiet the entire time.

I think she enjoyed the ride. She seemed content in her little basket.

My heart sunk when I saw my parent's house. It was covered in ivy. The windows were smashed in the front and the door was ripped off the hinges. They thought there was something here, they kept trying. I checked each room. No blood, no scraps of skin. My parents weren't here when they first attacked. They were probably out eating dinner or something. The house is covered in mirrors.

They couldn't have stayed here very long if they survived the first onslaught. My parents had a cat, Sassy. She must have left. The food and water bowl are empty. I hope she is okay.

I was able to grab some canned goods from the pantry even though most of them were gone. My parents said that in the event of an emergency, we could retreat to my grandparent's farm in Long Prairie. Hopefully, they're up there since my parent's little black Corolla is gone.

Snowy and I are sleeping in the crawl space along the side of the house. I brought a candle to light. This is where my dad used to store the Christmas tree and the ladder. Things are scrapping against the house. I'm almost positive it's those things that hunted me earlier.

I hear screaming. I need to stop writing and blow out the candle.

Day 11

There's more noise in this neighborhood.

I didn't sleep well last night. Gunfire, explosions, and a steady orchestra of screams went on continuously throughout the night. Sitting in absolute darkness while the world's on fire isn't easy. Sometime in the early morning, a woman came screaming up to the crawl space. She said she saw me go in there earlier and to let her in. I was about to open the crawl space, but her voice abruptly died. I heard a gurgle and snapping sound.

When I went outside this morning, there were fingernail marks on the outside of the door; there was blood too. It was everywhere.

I'm sorry.

Up the street, I noticed something was on fire. I could smell plastic burning and there was a cloud of smoke rising from an old brick school. I left a few notes for my parents, saying I was still alive and that I loved them. My dad's gun was gone. I hope they made it away safe. I packed a few extra things and closed the doors to the house. The windows were still broken on the front of it, but there's no point in repairing them. The monsters would know someone was living there.

It took me four hours to get to Little Canada.

The apartment building they lived in was completely destroyed. It was a three level apartment with simple blue hallways and white rooms. The apartments had been slashed and carved out by those things. There were pools of dried blood everywhere. The place stunk of rotting people. With no place to run or hide, they must've been easy targets here when the drum started. In her apartment, I found no signs of struggle, strangely. Hopefully, she was out shopping. I know she was going to cook curry that Friday night when it all started. They would've needed ingredients for that.

I'm going to start riding again here soon. I don't want to get caught out in the open when the drum begins. The refugees I saw yesterday were easy prey. Leaving the cities wouldn't be wise; there is no place to hide out there. I'm going to hide in the crawl space again. Snowy seems really tired. I imagine all these things are wearing on her too.

I know she misses the old world too.

Day 13

I haven't been able to write for a day.

I got caught on the road while trying to take a detour to my parents. I just now got back.

On my way back from Ling's apartment, a green line of twenty military vehicles came down 694 going west. There was a bulldozer in front of them, plowing aside each abandoned vehicle. All the vehicles were covered in ivy. Some were so tethered to the ground they had to push them multiple times. Walking behind them were men and women of all ages. They said they were mounting a counterattack in Minneapolis in a week.

I might join them.

I looked for people I knew in the crowd. There was no one.

I went around the crowd and biked down Lexington Ave to Highway 96 as a detour. I was halfway down highway 96 when the sun begun to set and the drum started.

I had nowhere to go.

When the drum started, time stopped. Shadows grew behind each car and tree. Streetlamps flickered with light, and then blinked to life. There was an eerie howling sound that filled the air. The drum sounded louder out in the open. Much louder, like actual living thunder. I got off my bike and hid it beneath a torn-apart pickup truck. We ran to the forest off the road. A shredded Semi had fallen into it. There was a gaping hole on its side. I started to crawl through the opening, when it appeared. The trailer was full of overturned boxes. I jumped in, trying not to look at it. It was

33

completely dark inside. Something dark and cloudy jumped in after me. I could hear its heavy walking on the floor. It smashed and shook the walls. Things were thudding into the boxes all around me. I could see its golden skeleton and curved claws thrashing. It was trying to get close to me. I fired my shotgun till it was empty. The first three shots did nothing, the last two made it curl up and fade into the wall. I pushed through the boxes and found Snowy crying. After stacking the boxes into a clumsy tower, I climbed out of the trailer.

They were covered with long black thorns.

We ran into the woods without looking back. They would come to collect the body, just like Gerald said. We hid all night in a drain pipe next to a highway pond.

We didn't sleep. We hardly breathed.

Day 14

Last night, I slept beneath the stairs in my parent's house. It was dusty and cramped, but I was able to build a wall out of boxes. I didn't want to keep using the same spot more than twice. This area is too thick with them. There were more screams. How can people think of moving to places they've never been? That's how people are getting killed. They don't know where to hide.

I got lucky inside that Semi.

I shot that monster at point blank range five times and it barely went down. I was just lucky to get it in such a narrow spot. The concept of the army firing into the night against these things is frightening. No wonder we haven't seen anything out of the armed forces.

I spent the morning doing one final exploration of my parent's house. I found an old radio that needed some batteries. It was sitting in my old room beneath a few blankets. I like to think my parents left it for me. I took a couple pictures of my family also, I hope they don't mind. My sister is living in Los Angeles. That place didn't need a steady storm of monsters. Not that any did.

I left my parent's house around noon. The bike ride home was eerie. The sun was hot and the sky cloudless. There were crows and seagulls cawing restlessly. Dogs picked at the empty cars and backpacks along the highways. I kept Snowy in the basket. I was being as careful with her as possible. Miniature Dachshund's were already fragile dogs. I don't know how she survived falling into that Semi.

*If it weren't for her I don't know what I'd do. I usually fall
asleep at night petting her.*

*When I was walking up the entrance ramp to Highway 100, I
found a grizzly sight. There was an endless smear of blood
blanketing the highway. Ripped dark clothing, pieces of skin and
hair, and smashed weapons were everywhere. Some troops must've
camped out in the open thinking they'll be okay. I managed to
rummage a black pistol and M16 out of the pile. I have no idea how
to use them.*

*The greatest strategy of these things might be that they can
be killed. Those pieces of hope we cling to with our guns is the
greatest bait imaginable. They use hope as a weapon. There are
more to these monsters than we think.*

Day 15

My house hadn't been bothered while I was gone. The doors were still locked and the windows still intact. Some houses that had been fine when I left for my folks had their windows broken and doors smashed in. That type of destruction didn't match the method of the monsters. Could it be something new? Luckily, my house is covered by the tipped maple tree so it looks destroyed.

But that didn't stop them a week ago. They came inside my house. I'll never forget the weight on the ceiling.

It felt good to be home last night for the drumming, even if I was crammed beneath the stairs. There were no screams or explosions, just the constant shaking of my house. Not a single shadow blocked the moonlight that falls into the basement.

I spent most of the morning consolidating supplies and refilling water. Plumbing still works, but nothing else does. It's still flowing strong.

Every day has been muggy and hot. Snowy and I have been drinking water nonstop. We're going to need more containers, but I don't want to ransack any houses or spook someone holed up with a gun.

I still have plenty of dog food for Snowy, but all I have left for my food are pantry goods. I have plenty to last me, but I'm tired of them. Everything tastes like metal now.

I went down to talk to Gerald this afternoon. He was really happy to see me. He actually cried a little bit when he saw me. We talked about what I had noticed with the monster, the army, and the survivors. The army had plenty of weapons, but needed more hands. Gerald knew this, but he doesn't trust the army. He said that they tried to recruit him and a few other people living around here. After that, almost everyone left. Only he and I were left in five block radius. As he told me this, I noticed a hint of depression on his face. I changed the subject and showed him the guns I'd found. He knew how to shoot the pistol, but not the M16. The recoil and sound knocked him off his feet and sent the bullets into someone's second level window.

We laughed the rest of the afternoon.

Day 16

It happened sometime in the early morning, which is sort of close to when the drum normally stops.

There was a long orchestra of gunfire near my house. I couldn't tell what direction it came from, but it couldn't have been very far. There were no screams between the metallic pops, just the endless drumming. The gun must've been something automatic with a big magazine. I lost track of how many bullets were fired. When it stopped, there were no other sounds except the drum.

Maybe, those things lured that person out of their home. They've probably been watching us during the day through reflections, and noting our locations for at night.

Nothing is going to feel safe again.

Before I walked to see Gerald, I took some extra time to make sure nothing with a clear reflection was visible in my house. I had already been doing this after the experience with the mirror, but I need to keep vigilant. If they are able to hide themselves in reflections without the drum sounding, then what else could they do?

The rest of the morning I spent moving empty boxes from the basement upstairs and rotating things around. I wanted to move food and clothes into the basement, but I was afraid of changing too many things. They might come back to scout the house for survivors. Using empty boxes and cans, I can give the illusion that nothing has changed.

I could hear my girlfriend and father calling me paranoid in the back of my head. They always thought I was too careful before the drum. I guess it's paying off, now? The irony is sickening.

Gerald seemed alright. I suggested the idea of exploring one house, and he was up for it. We choose a white rambler with slashed walls and broken windows. The house was across the street from Gerald. He said nobody had moved from it since the first night. We loaded our guns and inched through the shattered doorway. There was nothing alive inside. No pets. No people. There was blood on the brown carpet, a wide blob of it. A family of four used to live there. Gerald had to leave the home.

I looked around and found canned goods, bottled water, and toilet paper. I went in the basement and found nothing, but noticed a mirror on the inside of the basement door. A tall shadow was watching me in the darkness. It was wide, flowing, and had no face.

I ran out of the basement.

MIRRORS

Day 17

They came in my house last night.

I was downstairs, behind my wall of boxes, when the drum started. There was an immediate smashing of the door followed by a prickling of glass on my wooden floor.

They didn't waste any time. They knew exactly where to look.

The floor ached and buckled as they moved across my living room. There was more than one. The door to my basement had a lock on the outside. I wanted to barricade the door when the drum first started, but I knew that would be suspicious. They would know that someone was down here trying to hide. Snowy started to whine when she heard the floor boards bend. I whispered to her that she didn't have to worry.

They didn't want to kill her.

It took a few minutes of scuffling and smashing before they made it to the basement. I covered my dog's mouth and pointed my shotgun at the boxes. The wall of junk looked real to me, but who knew how particular their observations would be.

If this was the end, I'd fire every shot into the darkness. They kill quick and without mercy. It'd be a fast death.

I heard them walk up to the wall. Their bodies were scrapping against things, knocking things over as if they couldn't control themselves. The clatter would have been comical if the situation weren't so dire.

They didn't pause at the wall or give it a second glance. I watched them through the moonlit cracks in the boxes. I wanted to see more of them, but it was so dark.

There were two of them. The smaller one was more shadowy and harder to focus on. It had a white face, but I couldn't recognize any details to it. I recognized that gold skeleton beneath its shadow. The big one looked bulky, like there was some sort of hidden armor to its form. It had a long fleshy colored claw that dragged on the ground, like a strip of uncooked meat. It looked obscenely crude in comparison to its fabric-like body.

They paced around the basement, like two violent clouds. After scouring every surface, they left in one quick flurry.

I didn't sleep the rest of the night.

I spent the morning surveying the damages and moving things around. I couldn't fix the front door or window. They'd know I was here. I'd have to reevaluate my living space.

This is quite the price to pay for a reflection.

Day 19

I haven't been able to journal recently, not since they broke into my house a few days ago. They tore open the doors, smashed a window, and almost buckled in the floor. I couldn't fix anything. I couldn't clean anything. There could be no trace of interference.

They would know I was here.

The house was completely open now. I felt violated and unsecure. The monsters only came out with the drum, but the open door meant any passerby could waltz right in for supplies. They'd find me and my dog. They might have guns and get nervous. There might be a shootout.

I know those situations are on the horizon.

I must have security in my own home. My dad said a while back that when the basement was remodeled by my Uncle, the Beaver Board he installed as walls was never insulated. I cut a piece out, behind my false box wall, beneath the stairs. There was enough empty space between the wall and foundation for me to turn around or walk.

It was perfect.

I could hide away even further behind my wall of boxes. I could crawl inside and lay down. I'd replace the wall from the inside. They'd never know the difference. The bricks were a little cold, but I could put blankets up to insulate everything. There were a ton of bugs running around. The soil wasn't far away. I sprayed the place at least four times with insecticide. Bugs had gone wild since the drum had started.

I cut out other portions of the walls throughout the basement. Each one I marked with small piece of clear tape. I stored food, water, books, and photos. I didn't want anyone to walk inside and loot the place. It's sad to worry about such a thing in this situation.

I told Gerald that they almost got me. He said I could stay with him. I told him that wouldn't work, I couldn't endanger him. Secretly, I knew he wasn't being as careful as me. As lonely as I was, I couldn't take that chance.

Tonight will be my first night behind the wall. Snowy seems to like it fine. She gets so terrified with the drum though, she'd sleep anywhere. I haven't really slept since they came down here that night.

The weight of them walking, it was the most unforgettable sound.

Day 20

Last night was my first time behind the wall. The air was dusty, humid, and cloudy. I found an old battery-powered camping lantern. The white light on the sterile concrete made it look like we'd been buried in a catacomb.

The drum was just as loud as normal behind the wall, it seems like nothing can escape the sound.

I couldn't tell from behind the wall whether or not they came in my house at all. Not knowing is just fine with me.

I spent the morning moving the last of my supplies into the walls in the basement. I put up extra blankets and pillows inside the wall. I also moved more pictures and books inside. I want my hiding spot to be as cozy as possible.

I filled water till about noon. The plumbing's still working strangely; it's the only modern convenience I have left. I haven't used my IPod at all, or my laptop. I'm saving the batteries for when I really need an emotional pickup.

That'll be coming shortly; the world has been torn inside out. It's starting to wear me thin.

I saw Gerald in the afternoon. He said that the only message on the radio was a garbled and static-filled sentence about the counterattack in Minneapolis. There was no other transmission. He said there used to be a warning to get outside the cities. Now there was just the sole message about the counterattack and nothing else. Gerald was annoyed at the lack of details from the radio and anyone that had passed through. The federal government was silent, so were the local authorities.

Gerald said this wasn't even our world anymore when the drum started.

We walked further down the neighborhood. There were no people, no dogs, not a single thing moved beneath the ivy and howling leaves. We came across a tall brown house with a truck turned over in the driveway. The door was torn off fifty feet away. The front seat was covered in plants and dried blood. A severed white arm was attached to the black steering wheel. It stunk in the midday heat.

Gerald vomited. I didn't.

We walked further down to a North Hospital, which sat in the center of our neighborhood. The entire building had been covered in ivy and blue flowers. The doors to the attached parking ramp had been shorn off in metal slashes. A hospital had to be full of supplies.

We decided to explore it tomorrow morning after the drum had stopped.

Day 21

The drum stopped around Six AM. Gerald and I immediately met up outside my house. I decided to bring Snowy along, much to Gerald's dismay. He thought she'd get in the way. He said that I should have a big dog in this situation, not a small wiener dog.

I told him to be more secure with himself.

We went in the front doors of the hospital. There were smashed ambulances and police cars inside the turnaround. The sliding automatic doors had been shattered and torn off their tracks. Ivy had grown into the entrance and taken over the wooden concierge. We could see well enough in the lobby with the sunlight. The hallways to the elevators and stairs were completely dark. We both had flashlights. Mine was small and black, and taped to the end of my shot gun. A girl with Down Syndrome had given me the flashlight during Christmas last year at the bank. I would take those cheap suckers you give kids and rubber-band them together into a bouquet for her.

I wonder if she was still alive.

We found broken glass and blood everywhere as we explored the hospital. The hallways were full of reflective surfaces. We made sure not to let our flashlights linger over them as we walked. The monsters already knew we were alive, which was a depressingly real acceptance. Still, we didn't want to walk through the hallways being examined by pale, faceless shadows.

I carried Snowy in my backpack when we walked up the stairs. There was too much random debris and I didn't want her to fall. There was blood along the walls, huge smears of it. People must've have been trapped inside with them.

What a place to be when the drum started.

We explored the top two levels and didn't find anyone or anything. The halls were dried with blood. There was a mess of furniture, tools, stretchers, and papers around each corner. The ICU was empty, along with the cardiac wing. There were no pictures, emergency lights, or signs of occupation. The supplies were either smashed or absent. Gerald realized that when the army came through here, they had probably raided it for the upcoming battle. The hospital didn't look raided though, it looked completely mutilated.

There was no mercy here.

The exploration was extremely tedious, even with Snowy running to each room as our little scout. Plus, it was over a hundred degrees inside the hospital. We decided to explore the basement and main level tomorrow

When we left the hospital, I thought I heard a banging sound in the basement.

I hope it was just my imagination.

Day 22

Gerald and I met up again this morning, after the drum was done. He said his house shook last night against their weight. They knew he was alive, which meant they knew I was too. I couldn't tell if they came inside my house. Behind that wall, next to the foundation, it wasn't easy to hear.

Gerald still wanted to explore the hospital. He had guts.

The hospital was almost exactly the way we left it. The only change was the ivy had grown darker along each shape, like the plants were tightening their leathery grip. We had the basement and lobby left to explore. The lobby trailed back to the emergency room. There, we followed a long corridor into a wide chamber with a honeycomb of small rooms. Everything was completely dark, except for a few exit-sign batteries, which hadn't gone out.

I wonder how long they will last.

As we did yesterday, I kept sending Snowy to each room ahead of us. She strangely obeyed my points and head nods. Obedience was typically a dormant trait in Snowy. I like to think that she understood the situation. Life had become more serious for her. The monsters didn't bother with dogs, but there was still danger everywhere.

Humans were their chief prey. I'm jealous of my dog's favoritism.

The moment we finished exploring the main level of the hospital, the banging started. At first neither of us wanted to go down the stairwell. The banging was loud, metallic, and carried into every bloody wall and dead fixture. After a lengthy and heated conversation, Gerald convinced me that survivors might be trapped below.

The basement was a long hallway with a concrete floor and fenced in rooms. Boxes were thrown everywhere. The wiry tunnel started to collapse in around us when walked. At the end of the hallway were big metals doors latched together with a two black crowbars. Snowy immediately started to whine. The banging sound echoed everywhere as we walked. The windows in the center of the doors had been shattered. Two long, veiny arms with jagged gold blades hung out lazily.

It was one of them, in the daylight, without the drum thundering.

It heard us coming and started banging the doors wildly. We didn't stop to stare. I wanted to, but Gerald and Snowy ran. It let out a hiss as we fled. The sound surrounded us, like there were thousands waiting in the shadows.

Before I left, I wrote on the basement door in the stairwell: "Warning, there is a devil down here."

Day 23

Last night, I heard nothing but the drum. It's been quiet for a while now. There haven't been any screams, gunfire, or explosions; only the drum with its beating monster heart.

The lack of other sounds is calming, but also concerning.

How many people are left since the first night of the drum? It's been over three weeks now since everything happened. I've scouted my parent's. I've scouted Ling's apartment. I left notes for both.

Nothing is happening, nothing is moving. The world is in a continuous state of shock.

My food pile was starting to run low. I've cut back to two cans of food a day. I've only got about twenty left. I'm tired of soup and cold vegetables. The metal taste taints everything. What I wouldn't do for a greasy burger or a pile of chicken nuggets. I'm going to start breaking into houses looking for food. I don't care if the monsters see me or not. I need to stay on top of my food and water. I know the plumbing will go any day now. I hate worrying about it. Anxiety dictates all my thoughts these days.

I suppose being hunted on a nightly basis by faceless monsters will do that.

I made Gerald go with me when I broke into the house next to me. Nothing had moved on either side of me since the drum began. The house on my right had bleached stucco with a collapsed red roof. The door was already torn open. Inside there were no signs of death or struggle. A family of five lived here. They must've been gone when it started. I found some canned goods and split them with Gerald. We also found some toilet paper.

That's one luxury I was going to hold onto as long as I can.

After we gently pillaged the house, we sat around till the evening. I tried to talk to Gerald about my life before the drum, but he wasn't interested. He teased me about losing weight. I had lost close to 20 pounds since the drum started.

Gerald thinks the monsters are aliens or something. I don't think so. He said they attacked us already knowing how we would react. He said they must've been watching us for a while. I don't think they're aliens. He also said it could be the end of days. The devil had come for earth. I didn't believe that either. A biblical apocalypse wouldn't take this long.

The drum just started, time to stop writing and put out the light. Snowy is whining in her sleep. I never heard her do it, until this green hell, and the drum.

Day 24

I heard them last night. They came inside my house. I heard every wooden thump, every predictable smash. It took them two days to the trace the hospital back to me. It took Gerald only one day. Since I've moved behind the wall I haven't been able to hear much. Last night I could, like they wanted me to notice.

They wanted me to know, they'd seen me.

I spent the morning breaking into another house. The house was all boarded up along the windows with plywood. It was tall, white and full of windows. Whoever owned it must've been wealthy and probably had a bunch of food. Gerald told me not to go in that one. He said that people had been living there after the drum. The door was torn off just like mine. That's the sign of slain survivor. Gerald wouldn't go inside with me.

I've noticed he's had a harder time going inside houses and pillaging. Why has it gotten easier for me?

Inside the house it was the same scene. Smashed furniture, torn walls, and bloodied carpet. When I went inside, Snowy started sniffing a door in the entryway. There was crying and someone talking. Snowy started scratching on the door and whining. Someone yelled "Leave us alone, there is no food here." It sounded like a little girl. They must've stayed hidden when the monsters realized the boards were up on the house. Their parents must've been killed hiding their children. If my neighbor hadn't made the mistake of boarding up his house, I would've done that too.

I left a few cans of food outside the door.

Gerald and I once again spent the rest of the evening talking about the monsters. I hope this doesn't turn out to be a routine. I can't focus on them this much. They already dictate everything I do. I feel so much rage. I'm powerless. Everything I know is gone, like it was a half-awakened dream. The type where you wake up in the morning and can't tell reality from the dream you were having.

I haven't written about me that much, not since I've started writing in this memo pad. Before the drum I was a bank teller, a boyfriend, a son, and a friend. Now I'm just a survivor, a pillager, a coward who hides from nearly invisible monsters. My dog whines at me sometimes. She has food and water.

I don't know what she wants from me.

Day 25

Today was a good day. The counterattack is coming in two days. People have started walking through the neighborhood to assist, and are moving down Washington Ave, just beyond Broadway where I am. There are hordes of them; men, women, and children. The survivors fluctuate from dirty to clean, from well-dressed to ragged. Some carried weapons, others pushed wheelbarrows, and others rode on bikes. I was happy to see them for one specific reason.

I knew one of them.

My good friend Rick Craig was passing through with the droves. He had survived the drum. He had survived the weeks of hiding. He knocked on my door frame casually and asked if anyone was home. Snowy and I came running out full speed.

It felt so good to see the big loser, I can't even express it.

Rick had been a good friend of mine since high school. He had majored in engineering at St. Cloud State while I went to Anoka Ramsey. We still kept in touch though. He had just been over at my house a week before the drum had begun. He said he was starving. I brought him down to the basement to give him some food.

I didn't want people to see that I had supplies. There were lots of sweaty guns and hungry eyes walking by my house. I hope Gerald was safe.

Rick looked pretty decent for the entire calamity that'd been occurring. Like me, he'd lost a bunch of weight. Before the drum he was sporting a beer-belly and was pale as printer paper. Both physical conditions were due to his obsessive video game habits. Now he was tan, thin, and weathered, just like me.

Rick said that he looked for his parents and brothers. He was the oldest in his family. They'd been killed though. He found the house shredded and full of caked blood. He said he hid inside, unable to move or think. Other survivors told him about moving out of the cities. He couldn't leave his parent's house. Eventually, he got a radio working and heard about the counterattack. He said the army had plenty of guns but not enough hands.

I'll wait a day before telling him how foolish it is to join the counterattack.

Gerald came by later in the day and I invited him downstairs. We ate more canned goods, drank a little from a bottle of vodka I had left, and even played some cards.

It was a good evening.

Day 26

The bliss of having someone from my past in my life again was short-lived.

Rick spent one more night with me inside the wall. He was nervous despite me being completely awake and armed. He was sweating profusely behind the wall, which I was surprised about. The concrete foundation was cold and sterile. It was a cave. The walls were still cold and breathing, even in this early summer. I was living inside a cave inside a house. I hate the irony. The world was already warped before all this happened. Now our homes were nothing but beacons for them.

Our homes were now friendly traps, with memories and nostalgia as the bait.

The night passed to the constant hammer of the drum. I thought there would be screams and gunfights with the crowd coming through, but it was just the drum, the sole nightmare. Rick talked in his sleep in small wispy whimpers. He's bent by grief and rage. I'm worried it defines him now.

I'm worried everyone will become this way, even me.

I spent the day relating my tale to Rick. I told him about traveling, my parents, and Ling's apartment. I told him about the monster inside the Semi and the gunfight. He knew about the shadows in the reflections, he said in some parts of the cities people had painted warnings about them on garages and walls. The entire morning Gerald and I filled Rick's head with all the hideous things that had happened. Rick was bent on joining the counterattack.

Gerald and I told him it was ridiculous to fight these things in the open with groups of people. Rick said that the army had ways to beat them, to fight back. He said they'd have air support and machine guns planted across the skyscrapers.

He left around noon. I begged him not to go, and that it was suicide, and it was going to be a slaughter in the alleys. We're no match for these monsters, not fighting together in the open field. Rick wouldn't listen, he had too much rage. Now he was gone. Gerald told me not grieve over it, not to worry. He said the army might workout, maybe Rick would be right. Up to this point he said the counterattack was horseshit.

I'm writing behind the wall. It feels empty, even if Rick was just here a few nights. The drum thunders above.

Tomorrow, they'll start the counterattack.

Tomorrow I might go.

Day 27

It seems illogical to write now with the monsters and bullets. I want my voice down on paper in case the end comes. Snowy is shivering beyond belief. She is sitting on my knees, looking at me with those black eyes. The thundering bombs and splitting metal immobilize her. Why did I bring her? I should have left her with Gerald? Why do I always make stupid mistakes? Now we're trapped on the freeway waiting to be attacked by them, or hit in the fiery crossfire.

I shouldn't have gone after Rick.

I spent the entire morning biking to downtown via Broadway and Washington. Ivy had eaten most of the highway and side streets making the ride bumpy and uncomfortable. Closer to the city I followed a line of crushed vehicles, which had been pushed the aside by the army's bulldozers.

The line of rubble was endless.

The skyscrapers were covered in ivy from the top to bottom. They glowed in the hot sun, like the weeds were beaming about their latest accomplishment.

I found a rally of sorts. Troops were handing out weapons and supplies to every open hand. People were jumping up and down like it was some sort of rave. I didn't see Rick or anyone I knew on the crowded outskirts. I expected the attack to be more professional and organized.

Not a kamikaze concert.

They had set up a stage with some big black speakers. An old uniformed man spoke to everyone in a calming deep tone. The plan was to lure as many of the monsters in as possible and kill them. That was there plan, nothing else.

I left immediately for home.

I got to the freeway when the drum started. It started early, like it knew this would be happening tonight. I hid my bike and went inside a broken down clothing store for cover. Jets wailed overhead firing their cannons. Something exploded in the building next to me sending a shattered brick wall down on the desk we were beneath. They must've been mortaring the outside parts of the city.

Humans were going to kill me?

Snowy and I ran out of the building and down the freeway. A fighter jet flew overhead being chased by something black and shadowy. It looked like a piece of endless fabric, with a white face leading it. It caught the grey fighter jet, which was arcing away from the buildings. At that high speed how did that shadow fly? The cloud eventually caught the jet, which came apart in pieces and fell to the earth in fiery whacks. Snowy outran me down the freeway bridge and that's when we came across this destroyed hummer.

Things are walking around us. I'm going to hide us with a blanket.

Day 28

We spent the night in that fucking Hummer. I hated them before the drum. I thought they were selfish and ugly, but now I loved them. The monsters were all around us. Their shadows would brush against the car in the orange streetlights. The shapes moved so fast, it was hard to tell whether it might be the wind. I could feel there weight shake the car frame as they brushed against it. They had to have looked inside it? Hard to believe a brown blanket saved my life. Snowy didn't move the entire night either, that helped.

For about an hour there was a constant string of explosions. Small, big, echoing, quick, and constant bursts filled the air. There was spurts of bullets too, tons of them, a constant peppering of steel claps searing the air.

Then there was the drum, silence, and some cackling of fire.

In the morning, Snowy and I explored the city. There wasn't much to see. The smell of blood and smoldering oil was suffocating. The sky was the same blinding blue, the air was humid, and the ivy glowed everywhere. Blood was on the ground, rubble, and lampposts. It was even thrown up on the sides of buildings in random smears. Dogs howled and barked restlessly in the alleys. Ammo cartridges and casings clanked under our feet. Tanks sat smoldering, machine gun nests were destroyed, and a variety of black guns peppered the green pavement.

There were no bodies anywhere, just piles of red-stained clothes and shoes. I looked for remains of Rick, or any clue to his whereabouts. There was too many though, there was a pile or collection of pulverized flesh around every street corner. Smoke billowed in black clouds from a variety of shattered buildings. Closer to the skyscrapers, where the rally had been, was completely covered and full of smoke that I couldn't even get close.

Who knows how many people were killed last night.

I biked home slowly that afternoon. I picked up a few clips for my M16 and some shotgun shells. I found a few canned goods in the rubble. I spilt them with Gerald when I got back. He was happy to see me and surprised. I told him what happened, specifically the monster in the air that tore the fighter plane apart at high speed. He laughed about that.

He said the monsters thought of everything.

Day 29

Last night was quiet. Only the drum boomed, nothing else challenged it. I figure anyone who was still alive in the area besides Gerald and I were maimed or killed in the counterattack. The radio has gone silent. Gerald was disappointed. He said even if it was repeating the same message that meant someone was behind the speaker. The idea of complete radio silence doesn't bother me as much for some reason. When the plumbing finally stops, that'll be the last convenience linked to how things were.

The world becomes less recognizable each morning.

The vines, leaves, and grasses are flooding the streets and houses. On the ivy, small purple flowers continue to grow. I know nothing about plants, so this could be a typical species or not. Gerald says it something new, that the monsters are using the ivy for something. The overgrown plants appearing with the monsters and drum cannot be discounted. That was the only theory I believed out of Gerald. Despite my affinity for the man, most of his ideas were strange, vague, and rooted in some odd paranoia. Typically he'd trail of in the middle of his sentence and look around at the trees all wildly.

Still, any company was good company.

Whatever the case, the only plants I sort of remember are the bluebells I'd pick when I was kid. My mom would let me wander in the backyard while she read or sewed. I'd pick a bundle of them and put them in a small red cup. I'd always leave it on the edge of the patio table where she worked, hoping to surprise her.

I never asked if it ever surprised her.

I'm taking the day off from raiding houses. Rick probably being dead has taken a lot out of me. I spent the afternoon just sitting outside. I could've restrained him, or knocked him out? He would still have wanted to fight them though, to march off into the night with his little rifle held high. I could've slipped him a sleeping pill or something. He would still have gone. It's what the monsters wanted. They are mortal to give us hope, but immortal to kill us. Now he's dead and the drum still sounds, how important was that?

Tomorrow, I'll stand in a mirror.

It won't be here, but someplace else. I want them to see me. I want them to know I'm still alive. I want them to know I won't wander off into the darkness to meet them. I'm no fool. I'm no fool.

Day 30

Last night was nothing. More drum, it's the same every night. I'm not even scared anymore. I mean, there are tense moments behind the wall and all. A random thump or solitary scream will sometimes eek downstairs. I just grip my shotgun tighter. Snowy sleeps through all of it. Occasionally, her big black eyes will open from beneath the blankets and she pushes her head out to look at me. I always smile at her and whisper, "I'm still here."

If it weren't for her, they'd have me, I know it.

This morning I spent some time just walking through the top level of my house. I was never up there anymore. I couldn't clean it, move it, or give any clue that I was still in the vicinity. Looking back to the first day home, it was so silly to clean up after Snowy.

I'm depressed that I care.

I wish I could clean everything up. Sweep the glass, pick up the broken hardwood floor, and stand the chairs and couches up. I've even toyed with the idea of cleaning up another open house like the one next to me. I could watch to see how the monsters reacted, to see how they searched it. The risk was too great though, it wasn't worth inviting them to my home on a nightly basis.

This afternoon I sat in my backyard and watched the cotton-willow seeds sail by. Gerald walked up to see me for once, which was refreshing in a strange sort of way. He has to do some work once in a while. He may not what to come by tomorrow.

Since today I went and looked in a mirror.

I went to the house down the block with the mirror on the inside of basement door. I held up a flashlight to it and looked at myself. I was tanner, thin, and my hair was completely wild. I looked like a homeless person sort of, only my clothes weren't ragged or worn. I'd been wearing mostly shorts and t-shirts since the drum started, it was too hot for anything else. The weather hadn't changed once.

It didn't take long for the shadow to appear. It hovered behind me, changing shape slightly as it drifted. The white mask was there, devoid of any detail. There was a whispering sound in the darkness, like someone was talking about me at the far side of a hallway. I smiled at them.

It wasn't so bad.

Day 31

I knew they'd come for me.

They came inside last night. They came downstairs and scratched around the very wall I hid behind. They found nothing, as you can tell. The moment the drum started I heard the floorboards creek above my head. New dust fell, which didn't seem possible since my house has ached and shook with each of their visits. I'm use to them sniffing around my basement and house looking for me. It's a bizarre level of comfort. Before, I wouldn't take my shirt off at the beach. Now, I hide from monsters on a nightly basis.

The level of irony stuffed into life is sickening.

In fact as these days, hours, and minutes stomp on; I can't help but notice the little ironies popping up everywhere. I've finally lost weight, but the world is ruin. I'm writing more, but my audience might be completely massacred. I'm finally a healthy tan and not a pale Irish Sheep Dog, but the there is nobody at the beach. It would've been nice to have made these changes in our old world. In these days I have no choice but to change.

My dad once said the only constant in the world was change.

Tomorrow, Gerald and I will finally start exploring houses again. We've taken a break recently and only because Gerald got all wish-washy about it. We'll have fewer issues entering houses for supplies. I assume most of the people that were hiding joined up with the counterattack. I think Gerald is running low on food also. He'd never tell me he needed some. He's got this weird silent pride

68

about him. He keeps getting skinnier though, and that's discouraging for such an old little man. The situation we're in requires honesty, why is he being so secretive?

There is one thing I noticed about last night that was a little strange. I heard the monsters come inside and rattle things around a little bit. However, I never heard them leave. Would they sit inside my basement the entire time? For an abominable fighting force that seems relatively human. Patience, observation, memory, these are all characteristics of a higher intelligence and not some shadowy bloodlust beast. I lose count of how many times I think of the monsters in a given day. What are they? Why are they doing this? I need to end this with something other than them. Sunshine and lollipops, and rainbows everywhere, and lots, and lots, of fun.

I think my dad use to sing that...

Day 32

Last night there were screams. Not many, not few, but a solid in-between number. It's been a while since we've had any screams, which is strange thing to notice, but all you can do is observe these days. Inaction is the only safety. The howls happened in the early morning. Before, when there was a steady string of shrieks, they'd typically occur in the dead hours of morning. People hide, but get anxious, then trying moving.

They get swallowed up in the darkness.

It's depressing, well, many things are, but specifically that people haven't learned about what's happening and adapted. I can invent three simple rules to follow right off the top of my head.

There are so few of us now, I can feel it in the silence and the swinging trees. They'll come for us every night until we're all dead and pulverized. What'll they do when we're all gone? They can't possible exist for our sole destruction. No creatures are that asinine or barbaric. They don't eat, harvest, or enslave us.

Is our death really their only concern?

Gerald and I explored a house today. The first one was a brown rambler with shattered windows. At first I got strange feelings about the place because there was an odd whistling sound coming from the door. We went inside anyways with our guns ready, and it was just the wind playing on the broken bits of glass. Every sound scares you these days. There was nothing there, not a thing. A bunch of the cupboards were opened and the basement had been torn apart. I assume some other survivors had come through looking for supplies.

I'm convinced we can try breaking into a store or market just outside the neighborhood. People may have pillaged them already, but I'm sure they don't have the manpower to take everything. There is a Rainbow Foods just down the street from us, or about a mile away. Tomorrow, we'll try looting. I don't think there are any authorities to enforce anti-pillaging laws.

I wish there was, I wish there was any authority.

In the house today, Gerald and I found a bloody wall and bed. It looked painted almost, like they'd taken pride in it. How many grim reminders do we need?

The world is just one green slaughterhouse.

THE ROAR

Day 33

*Today was a bad day. Gerald and I tried to explore the
Rainbow Foods at the south end of the neighborhood. We walked
down 81 to get there. The oceans of ivy weren't as strong on the
highways as they were on the neighborhood side streets. The plants
were so thick on some streets, you couldn't keep track of where the
pavement and leafy floor separated. Occasionally, your feet would
fall through the leather vines and pop onto the asphalt. The
missteps were completely unpredictable and irritating.*

*The moment we walked into the Rainbow parking lot we
knew something was up.*

*There were overturned cars blocking the entrance to the
grocery store. Just outside the leafy automatic doors, a few empty
machine guns sat surrounded by punctured sandbags. Nobody
manned the guns. The army must've tried to make this store some
sort of checkpoint.*

They had clearly failed. Nothing moved and nothing lived.

*We walked up to the entrance casually with our guns
hanging over our shoulders. It was slightly weird for us to carry
guns in the daylight when the drum wasn't thundering away, but
something in my gut wouldn't let me feel safe without the gun.
Gerald clearly felt the same way, since he brought his rifle
everywhere.*

It was a nice, unspoken paranoia between us.

*The moment we reach the curved sandbag wall there was a
popping sound next to Gerald's hunched back. More followed*

above and below us. Pretty soon we were surrounded by searing sand-ridden bursts. Someone was shooting at us with a silenced gun. They weren't trying to kill us, or else we would've been very dead. They were trying to warn us that this was their store.

That everything inside belonged to them.

We gave up and ran off. Snowy had to wait for us. The sounds really scared her. She could've easily outrun us home. We didn't look back to see where the shots might've come from. We didn't want to push the shooters charity. They could've killed us without a second thought.

Today is a sad day. We've already become savages. That really didn't take very long. Not long at all.

Day 34

This morning Gerald and I discussed what happened yesterday at the Rainbow Foods. People were already beginning to mark their territories and protect food sources. Why did people have to become so greedy? The situation we were in as survivors changes are priorities, but it shouldn't set back our morals.

I'd read all those apocalyptic stories and such, and there'd be chapters about how people turn on another. Cannibalism, fighting, and torture were a few post-apocalyptic issues you'd see in those books. I always thought they were just more plot devices for us to stagger through as readers.

It'd been nice to be wrong.

We decided to at least clear out the empty houses around us before exploring another major store. From what we could tell, nobody lived in our surrounding blocks except that one house with the children hiding. We would leave them alone until they came out. There was no point in scaring or acting like they were safer with us.

They could be much safer and smarter than us. We didn't want to be their end.

We explored ten houses. Eight of them showed no signs of struggle or habitation. We found a plethora of canned goods and dried food. In the last two we found a few bloody rooms with torn clothing and dried piles of blood.

I've grown immune to the smell of blood. Even if it's been simmering in the hot sun in this never-changing weather, the smell doesn't wrench my nose.

My mom had one of those super sniffers. One time a rotten potato fell between the counter and the wall at my parent's house. She easily tracked the sour smell like a middle-aged bloodhound. She'd be going crazy with all the smells drifting through the air. Oil, smoke, melted plastic and skin, and a sweet perfume smell that wrinkles out from the purple flowers in a wavy haze.

I wonder what it'll do.

Gerald and I ate dinner together. We've started talking about our past lives a little bit more. At the onset of everything we'd never really mention our families or friends. It hurt too much. Our old lives weren't that far away at the beginning. Now they were a world of fantasy and memory. I've noticed my dreams are featuring more and more people. My parents, my sister, my girlfriend, everyone really.

It's better than nothing.

Day 35

Last night, the drum sounded like usual, but it started and sounded later. If this becomes a pattern, I'm going to be very upset. The consistency of the drum allows us to survive and adapt. For the entire run of this rhythmic death-cycle we've been dealing with a consistent beat. This morning, for the first time ever, the drum ended when the sun was nearly at full strength.

I'm on edge from it. They could come at any moment.

Of course, before this happened, I had started sleeping through the night. For the first four weeks I wouldn't sleep very well at night. Now, I sleep like a baby behind my dusty wall. They could silently drift inside my house and I wouldn't even know. If they were loud enough to wake me up I'd go back to sleep. Snowy sleeps through it as well.

I wonder if she fears the monsters like I do. They have such a dark and sinking aura, I wonder if she feels it? She'd whine. She doesn't anymore.

Today, Gerald and I covered 12 more houses. Family pictures, scraps of skin, piles of hair, shattered televisions, tumbled bookshelves; basically, a whole collection of household destructions. All houses we've visited are starting to mesh together. A constant collage of household mangling.

The overgrown houses and overturned cars don't really alleviate the indoor images.

When is the weather going to change? Almost five weeks of this...

Day 36

Last night, I woke up to the most amazing sound. There was rain, a thunderous pouring storm. The falling water echoed hard enough to block out the drum. The sound was soothing and extravagant, like my mind was on vacation for a night. It felt so good not to hear the murderous beat, but real, snapping thunder.

My dog hates thunderstorms. She instantly started to whine. I pulled her close beneath the blanket. She eventually fell asleep, but only after a series of wheezing, labored breaths. I guess the drum hadn't changed her that much. The drum didn't bother her, but the thunder did?

It rained all day. Gerald and I were going to continue our scavenging. Instead, we called it off to enjoy the change in weather. A bubbling grey wall of clouds filled the sky. The sun was nowhere to be seen. I actually sat out in the storm on my steps despite the streaks of lightning. The humidity had increased tenfold inside my house. In the basement it was still cold though, nothing really caused the temperature to survive down there.

I've noticed my sensitivity to heat and overall temperature change has dropped through the floor. Maybe that's because all the fat has melted off me from my miraculous diet of canned goods. I'm so tired of that sterile metal taste. These dark times have made me physically a better person. Why did it take this? Why?

I sort of forgot about the rain and what it does.

Memory and nostalgia fall with every nibbling drop. The feelings of the past world sink into me, like an old song or something. I think of it falling off the roof at my parent's house, their farm, or even the neighborhood streetlights at night. Plenty of time these days to remember things; especially, about how everything was before the drum.

One time after a wedding, Ling and I ran through a downpour to a bar along the Mississippi river. The rain was so heavy it hurt us as we ran. I had an over-sized suit, and she had a purple dress that curled around her narrow shoulders. We laughed, and drank the night away against a backdrop of tropical music and overly sweet tropical drinks. She ran so fast back then. I thought I'd never catch her.

I'm not sure I like the rain.

Day 37

The rain and thunder stopped abruptly last night. The drum appeared quickly and deliberately, like it was jealous of the clout the thunder had. My chest became a little heavy when just the drum hammered the shadows.

The storm was a nice reprieve.

I've been worried about my thoughts recently, or my overall state-of-mind. I've been thinking far too much about the monsters. Maybe it's been these consecutive weeks of little or no confrontation with them which has caused it. I don't forget them. I don't forget that they are there. I'm wondering about them in general, or in a vague hypothetical way.

Earlier on, Gerald was fixated with them, and would talk about them every day for at least a few hours. It's like a disorder or syndrome based in curiosity. It follows the drum. I can't stop thinking about them. They're all I can think about besides my family. I don't know why they've been able to invade my thoughts, especially during the day when you can only find them lurking in reflections. Not my mind, not my curiosity.

If only I could see them better, take a picture or something. Their bodies look sharp and dangerous. From what I've seen, they have bones beneath their shadowy disguises; they're usually a faded gold with a grey and sinewy tissue holding them together. They have curled horns that change colors, and a white shapeless face with no specific features.

What could they be? Obviously, they're related to the plants, but what's the relationship? They're mortal, I killed one myself. It was hard to kill, exactly five point-blank shots with the 22.

They have weapons, but they're hidden beneath their cloaks. Usually, they have blades that are grafted to their skin. They throw thorns, too. Who knows what those do when they pierce you. There's a bigger version of them too, only their bones are a piercing red. They have an obscenely big arm that looks like an overextended strip of muscle. I wonder what it does. It's probably a hidden weapon.

I don't think I can keep hiding in the basement this frequently. I want to see them. I want to know them. To be hunted by invisible monsters night and night-out borders on insanity. The drum knows. The drum knows I'll eventually go out to it. I'll be drawn to the beasts.

This must be a tactic by them. I swear it.

Day 38

There have be countless times where I've had an ambitious plan all worked out. The moment I've taken action with this strategy, something small and insignificant has thrown me off track.

Well, at least this time I'm very legitimate in my laziness.

Just recently, I've become obsessed with the monsters, beasts, or demons that have been hunting us nightly. Last night, since things have been really quiet, I decided to try and explore, and the very least observe the night. I don't know why I have to do this. I just need to. I can't let them have it. I can let them have my hope completely.

Tucked away, behind the movable wall in the corner of my basement, lies my hiding place. The Beaver Board panel that I use to move in and out sits behind an adjacent wall of boxes. It's a great hiding spot, so if I leave my hiding place, I might give it all up. Weird how I've become so proud and protective of my secret places.

Behind the wall last night, I got everything ready. I loaded my 22, M16, and pistol. I packed a few grenades into my backpack with some spare ammo. I'd food the grenades while scavenging. I still hadn't used one yet. They looked pretty simple.

Before I went to remove the wooden panel that hid the empty wall from the world, I asked my dog if she thought it was a good idea to go outside. Beneath that pale blue lantern light her eyes shined and trembled, like she was going to cry. After a few seconds of severe guilt, I decided to use a spy hole I'd made at the other end of the wall. The hole was about a half-inch wide. It spied directly into the laundry room. A piece of black tape blocked it. I didn't want a shaft of blue light to bleed out into the room.

Something like that would give us away.

I put out the light before I went over to it. I peeled the tape back very quietly and looked through the hole leisurely.

I nearly pissed myself with what I saw.

One of them was there, lurking in the blackness. I could see its misshapen form shifting in and of out of the shadows, like time itself was freezing and unfreezing. The only bit of moonlight in the entire basement caught its golden bones, which shimmered against a rough white. Who knows how many nights it had been waiting for me to come out?

I didn't panic, or else I wouldn't be writing this entry. I was a prisoner, and I didn't even realize it.

Day 39

My nights of semi-peace have abruptly become nightmarish and anxious. Last night, knowing one of them was out there, I could barely breathe behind the wall. The entire time, I clutched my gun. The safety was even off, like I couldn't have one rational thought separating me from firing blindly through the Beaver Board. If I did manage to kill the one outside my hiding spot, many more would hear the shots—they'd swarm and tear me to pieces.

Inaction was constantly saving my life in this new world. In the old civilization, procrastination was constantly looked down upon or cherished. In hindsight, our modern life was full of ugly dichotomies. I'm not sure I'm far enough away from that world to judge it yet.

I'm getting there though.

I told Gerald about my new bunkmate. Understandably, he was pretty upset about the whole thing. He told me to leave the house and stay with him. I managed to talk my way out of it. I really don't trust his hiding spot. He's a little too lucky with the monsters.

Gerald has been seen in mirrors also, why haven't they started to camp out in his house every night?

The new green world radiated a ridiculous amount of heat today. Everything is so emerald and velvety; you could actually see the sun and moisture boiling off all the plants. My entire house has been covered with the ivy. New vines have popped up; they're thin, round, and bright green. There's no end to them when you look outside. Structures are vanishing behind their mossy shells.

Plumbing still works. I've got much more respect for plumbers now. I'm already looking forward to the rain coming again.

We explored the rest of the houses around us. We found plenty of canned goods inside of them. Found some dog food too. The stench from the kitchens we explored was disgustingly sour and stagnant. All the other food had rotted. Only the dried smell of blood managed to block it out. I'm not sure which one I would pick to smell on a regular basis.

I'll think about it.

Tonight, Snowy and I are going to try sleeping upstairs away from the wall. This is a risk I'm willing to take. If I make one false move behind the wall—I'm dead. Before, I had no idea there was one right outside. Now that I know, well, I'm a wreck. The closet door in my spare bedroom has been closed since everything happened. That's as good a place as any I guess.

If these journals stop, you'll know it failed. I'm almost to the end of this memo pad. I'll have to find a new notebook.

Day 40

It's hard to believe that an empty piece of foundation behind some paper thin 70's décor would be more comfortable than a closet. Well, it was, in fact my little basement hiding spot was much cozier than this small wooden cell I slept in last night. The heavy heat was ridiculous inside the closet. Snowy panted nearly the entire night. I went through a couple bottles of water. My eyelids were even sweating. I don't think that's ever happened to me before.

Despite the heat, I still heard it come inside my house last night. The moment the drum started thudding, there was a scratching sound outside the house, and then the floor creaked and shuttered. There was a hollow running sound down the stairs. It ran hard enough for the house to shake from where I was hiding.

I haven't felt vibrations like that for a while—another reason to like my original hiding spot.

I didn't sleep inside my closet. The whole experiment was for nothing. The whole idea that these things are inside my house waiting for me to make one misstep sickens me. Actually, sicken is sort of a passive word. A more accurate and aggressive word would be insanity.

I'm going to have to do something about it. I'm going to have to get them to leave.

Gerald and I talked about exploring more houses outside of our neighborhood. We'd need to explore the neighborhood more before breaking into any of them. The shooting outside of Rainbow Foods traumatized us, and now we're going to be extra careful before expanding our territory. I'm worried about it. We've got enough food for at least a few months, but if there are other survivors will they compete over food, too? I'd assume yes, considering what happened a few weeks ago with the sniper.

I'm writing this entry outside this evening. The sweet and damp air keeps curling the yellow pages. 40 days of this botanical hell. I'm starting to feel edgy, like I need to start plotting a way to get back at them. I want to travel, maybe get up to our farm in Long Prairie, but I'm too scared of being caught in the open again.

I feel like such a coward.

At least everyone during that counterattack tried to kill the monsters; they tried to take back what's ours. Granted, none of those people are probably still animated. The monsters are though; yes, they're very alive.

They're too real.

Day 41

I've come back to the wall. I couldn't take another night in that closet. I know it's out there waiting for me to breathe wrong, or to stumble and bump the hollow wall. I wonder if it knows how close it is to me. All it would have to do would be to stab into this ridiculous wall and skewer me. It could just leave me back here to die, and Snowy would be under Gerald's care.

I'm not sure he would care about her at all. He wasn't very patient with her when we explored the hospital. He'd border on screaming when she'd run off to explore attractive scents. With the constant aroma of rotting food and dried blood, I imagine there are plenty of good scents.

Even in this monster-ridden plant world, a dog seems like too much of an inconvenience for him.

I've got a plan for this monster that's cozied up in my basement. I've been saving the radio I found at my parent's house and it's batteries for when things get truly hopeless. Besides, Gerald gives me daily updates about the empty static that buzzes on every channel. I'm going to leave the radio on before the drum starts. I'm putting it in the house next to me between the walls and couch. I'll leave the volume up just slightly, just enough for them to be driven crazy by that fizzling buzz.

At least I think it'll drive them crazy—maybe. Their tolerance for insanity must be high considering what they do.

Gerald and I walked outside the neighborhood today; more hot wind, cloudless sky, and blooming green life everywhere. More broken homes with shattered windows. More ivy covered roads, and dangling trees flushed with leaves.

I'm tired of it.

Nothing moves along the roads. There are no vehicles, no lights, and no people bustling about. The sounds of planes are gone. The droll of the highway has vanished. All the emptiness sucks at your stomach, like an ugly thought hidden far away inside you.

The movies and books glorifying the freedom that comes with an apocalypse have never eaten canned goods for five weeks. They've never buried the pieces of strangers or taken dog food out of a bloody kitchen cabinet. They never counted how many cotton willow seeds drift in the hot air. Well, that last one was more realistic, so maybe they did.

That monster has to go. I won't let it haunt me. Everything else does—yes, everything.

Day 42

The radio didn't work.

The moment the drum started, I was listening for it against the flimsy wall, waiting for it to come downstairs. At first there was nothing, just the distant thunder of the drum. Then I heard it. There was a scuttling sound on the ceiling. A heavy walking followed, and the stairs suddenly thudded in the darkness. I watched it drift inside my basement like an armored, spiked cloud.

I want to see its face. I want to see it, no matter how hideous, no matter how discussing it might be. I have to see the face of these monsters.

I didn't see it though, not even close.

The monster, as if knowing I was watching it, never came close enough for me to see its face. I watched it all night. I watched that shadow seamlessly drift in place. It knows I'm here, but it can't find me, it can't conceive where I might be. In a way, I'm honored that they'd spend such a large amount of time looking for me. Of course, I don't think the monsters have any other hobbies.

They don't look built for arts and crafts.

The radio failed miserably. I found it still on between the wall and furniture. I wasted all that battery power for nothing. I was hoping they'd at least pay a little attention to it. I didn't tell Gerald about my little experiment. He'd probably laugh at me, and then whistle off a few sly comments. Gerald's a good guy, and I'm grateful for his company, but he's a little too bleak about everything. I mean he's right, the world's very empty, despite the instant jungle that has sprung up.

Tomorrow, I'm going to explore outside the neighborhood some more, and see if I can find some dynamite. I might be able to rig something—like a trap. Hopefully, I don't kill myself in the process. If I leave some more enticing bait nearby, will the monsters go investigate it? They've got to have some sort of human weakness to them, maybe its curiosity. Almost all creatures have curiosity.

Clouds drifted through today. They were the first clouds I'd seen since that thunderstorm and before. They were bubbly piles of folded vapor, which threw long omnipresent shadows across the neighborhood in slow drags. The lack of sun had no effect on the plants. I loved it though; I was able to walk around my crushed house without sweating or squinting.

We take for granted the strangest things.

Day 43

I thought exploring outside the neighborhood would cheer me up a little bit. There might be some sort of social order, or sign of civilization retaking hold in another neighborhood.

There was nothing, just more of the same.

I didn't see anyone, not a single person out wandering between the green buildings. There was just emptiness, loneliness, a cicada soaked jungle where homes used to be. The roads, despite the ivy and simmering flowers were empty. The asphalt and cement that peeked out from the soft laced driveways, seemed lonely and empty—like it didn't know what to do with itself.

I imagine the homes are as lonely as the people who are forced to hide in them.

Houses were layered in ivy and flowers. It dribbled down the roofs like bright green flaps of skin. The hot wind jostled them in leathery clumps. They looked like old ramen noodles thrown over a fork. Trees were overburdened with thick leaves, to the point that they had tipped over, crashing on cars and walls. They trees were completely bent over, but their veiny roots still clung into the dirt, like the new plants were refortifying them. They're so affluent and wild now, like the world isn't remotely holding them back.

On one particular road, which looked like it had been travelled recently due to the fresh tread marks on the mossy ground—Snowy and I hid below a twisted car that was covered in ivy. I wanted to make sure nobody was watching or hunting me. I don't know why I was so worried. It just felt like someone was watching or following us. I wish I could read or call someone to confirm if I'm being paranoid or not. I'm not going to ask Gerald if I am. That'd be like asking a duck if I could fly. I'm not even sure that makes sense...

I listened and watched the wind as Snowy and I hid beneath the car. Cotton willow seeds and the petals off those purple flowers have flushed the air with debris. They waver and spiral on the hot air like someone was powering them, like an invisible hand shaking them back and forth. The leaves boil restlessly against the dropping heaves.

I'm tired of the roar. I'm tired of all of it.

My sister use to like weather like this. She really loved it. She'd sit on the screen porch at my parents and talk about it.

I imagine this new weather lacks the same charm.

Day 44

Last night, the monster wasn't there, or at least it was hidden to the point of complete invisibility. I have no idea what the damn things are, so that could very well be possible. I watched every shadow and slant of moonlight. I memorized every detail. If something shifted or glided in the darkness, I'd know about it.

Nothing though, not a single bit of movement.

I'm not sure if the monsters are capable of psychologically torturing us directly, or even strategizing to the point of manipulating our rampant paranoia. First, I had no idea they were even outside my hiding place—waiting for me to make the slightest error. Second, I thought setting up a radio in the empty house next to me as a distraction might get the damn thing out of my house. And now third, I've figure out that they will occasionally not even be there or remain hidden to simply test my shattered psyche.

Someone please tell me I'm giving them too much credit.

Today, again, there were more clouds than sky. The shadows hung on everything and the air was quiet beneath their dark cool drags. Gerald and I explored a few more houses. Inside each home, the plants had crawled in through the windows and siding. Ivy bled down from the ceiling in dark green drops which trembled against the hot drafts of outside air. The plant's devouring our streets and homes was disturbing enough from the outside, watching them worm their way into our homes quickly and ardently like some botanical plague—was even more disheartening.

Gerald keeps mentioning that we should start burning some of the plants to see how the monsters react. I was onboard with the plan at first, but what if the fires grow out of control? No firemen around; therefore, no way to contain a resilient blaze.

Still, it'd feel good to burn them up, and watch them sizzle to an uneven pile of fibrous ash. Just imagining the controlled burn makes me more relaxed.

We didn't find anything too interesting when we explored the houses. More canned and dried food for us to eat. We've both collected considerable stockpiles of each, which stays hidden inside our houses. The five block radius of our neighborhood has been completely explored and investigated. The homes we explored today, which were a pair of flat green ramblers, were the first two outside of our self-designated comfort zone. More exploration equals more risk, and not just from the monsters. The incident with the sniper outside of Rainbow Foods still weighs on our minds.

Tonight, I'll wait for the monster—like it waits for me.

Day 45

Last night, nothing came drifting downstairs. I waited patiently and quietly with the black nozzle of my M16 pressed against the wall. The monster never appeared. I'm not sure where it would've been. Eventually, the allure of stalking the stalker wore off and I fell asleep. Of course, I was sitting up with my sweaty face plastered to the Beaver Board wall. I woke up this morning when Snowy started to lick the slimy mixture of drool and perspiration off my face.

I wonder if she thought I was dead.

The nights have been silent recently, just the drum booming over and over again. At the onset of this slaughter, there were one-sided firefights, quick screams, provocative explosions, and the endless groans of airplane engines.

Now, nothing stirs the night, besides them and their drum. I never thought I'd miss the mayhem. I never thought I'd find the sounds of gunshots comforting. I remember sleeping at my parents' house next to the pond, which hosted the frogs singing in their scratchy symphony. It would drive me crazy. I'd literally yell at frogs in the middle of the night. I miss it now. I miss everything. Even those common modern annoyances of gridlocked traffic and piercing cellphone rings would be soothing at this point.

Gerald and I took a break today. The sun was back to full force with its searing bronze rays. Even though I'm completely tan now, I still feel like I was getting cooked beneath its heavy beams. A few days of clouds were a condensation sunk paradise. The shadows made a difference, even if their cool edges felt foreign, deep, and almost treacherous.

I blame them. I blame the monsters. Shadows will never feel the same again, I know it.

Tonight, might be the final straw, considering monster watching and waiting. Despite me losing a ton of weight from this metallic-flavored diet, I'm a nervous wreck when the drum plays. Knowing they're that close to me, just outside lurking behind some shoddy building material, well, it makes me sick. Hypertension, I'm sure I've got it. My heart beats ridiculously fast inside the foundation, fast enough that it feels like nothing beats there at all.

My chest has become empty, devoid that fist of muscle that recycles my blood. Also, I think I'm going crazy. That sentence might be identified as an oxymoron in more normal circumstances.

If my shadowy cloud of gold blades and ivory bones isn't here tonight, then I might just have to explore. I'll take Snowy with me too. I've had enough of this hiding game. This world isn't worth surviving in, if you've got to cower in the cobweb drenched crawlspaces of old.

Day 46

It was here last night. It'd probably been hiding inside this entire time. Last night, the drum started normally. I watched for it again, noting every subtle change to the shadows and blue moonlight. After thoroughly convincing myself that it wasn't there, that in fact nothing was there at all, I crept out of my hiding place behind the wall and boxes.

I dressed for the occasion. I wore a dark blue bullet-proof vest, which I found the night I was trapped out in downtown. The front of it had been slashed by one of their claws so badly that the Kevlar's top layer was shredded and dangling out like frizzy hair. I wore jeans with black combat boots I'd also found. For weapons, I carried my M16 and pistol, with plenty of ammo for both.

Yes, it was eerie taking these items off the dead. It helped that the bodies were completely absent, and only bloody, bile soaked smears remained.

It helped having no faces.

At first, it felt very strange exploring my basement at night. For so long I had just been a spectator during the night and the monster summoning thunder. Now I was in it. Now I was another shadow stalking the very things that hunted me. I had taped a flashlight to the point of my rifle. It beamed a small blue circle against the breathing darkness. Every shape seemed foreign to me, even if I had walked by them a thousand times in the daylight. Eventually, I made it to the stairs. I slowly tiptoed up the steps trying not to crinkle the old tan wood.

It was there. It was standing at the top of the stairs.

I didn't fire at first. The monster didn't move or twitch. I knew it was there. It's hulking shadowy drifted then solidified in the narrow doorway. What slight beams of light came through the house, trickled down its golden bones and claws in speckles of indecipherable illumination. I want to see its face. I want to see the face of these devils.

Thinking quickly, since I didn't want to fire my gun and attract a whole horde of these things to my basement, I grabbed a small plastic water bottle that was attached to my belt loop. I quietly placed the clear bottle over my guns nozzle and aimed it at the monster. I remembered this working in a Martin Scorsese moving I'd watched ages ago.

First off, the recoil of the M16 threw me off the stairs. The water bottle exploded sending an inconveniently placed spurt of water into my eyes. The monster whirled around surprised, and I imagine, confused, though I couldn't see any of its features. It leaped at me, a gleaming shadow of pointed blackness. It misjudged the distance though, hitting the low ceiling and collapsing through the stairs. Pieces of wood toppled down onto the beast, along with boxes and cleaning products. The thing wrenched about wildly, but the debris loosened its footing. I quickly pulled myself up, and fired into the pile of broken wood and ripped carpet.

My clip clanked empty, after what seemed a few seconds.

My tongue was heavy and I started to panic. I was one of them now. I was one of those sounds now.

A rattle of gunfire that goes quiet in the night.

Snowy started to whine. She knew what was coming. She knew they'd come for me. I fired my gun into one of the small, narrow basement windows that open to the back lawn. I knocked a bunch of glass onto the long grass with the butt of my rifle. Something creaked above my head. I just barely managed to get through the piled junk and rubble.

Snowy was inside the wall before I could even move. I was breathing hard and crying. Too close, too close to the end of it all. Who would take care of her after I'm gone?

They came in the moment I got the false piece of board into place. So many of them came in my house. The walls ached beneath them. Dust billowed out from the walls, ceiling, and strangely enough, the floor. Both versions of the monsters came down. The big ones with their long obscene arms and the smaller camouflaged ones, which I had just killed.

They didn't stay long. They followed the trail of glass outside the window. They also took the body silently away, not disturbing a single wall or broken stair. They came for their dead so quietly and gently, they have to feel things. I don't understand why they're doing this.

Day 47

Bruises have invaded my back and elbows. I didn't even know they could grow so fast. It looks like I've been blotched and decorated with a poorly mixed can of blue and red paint.

It took me all morning to pull the splinters out of my calves and ankles. That's the only spot those wiry brown shards punctured me. I'm not sure how that works. I'm just glad it wasn't those little black thorns they throw. God only knows what kind of poison waits inside those darts. Everything about the monsters, every detail and characteristic, happens to be for killing. I can only assume the same with their projectiles.

Thanks to the little battle I can no longer get out of my basement unless I crawl through that broken window. The stairs are now a pile of broken wood and smashed boxes. When the caravan of monsters came through the upstairs to retrieve their fallen soldier, their weight broke most of the floor, and their frames shredded the walls.

I think they were angry. I think they'll want vengeance. If they have problem-solving minds like ours, they're probably capable of complex emotions. Revenge. I know it motivates me. I'm glad I killed it. I want to kill more, and I will. They can't torture us like this, like we are nothing but insects.

Despite my paranoid fears, and one day removed from this debilitating fight, no monster waited inside my basement for me. I thought a whole horde of their spikey and shadowy cohorts would come floating down. Not one came, not a single beast. Was my trail of glass to the outside that convincing? Apparently, or at least sometimes, the ideas that are generated in panic happen to be the best ones.

I can't get overly comfortable. One brush against a reflection and those faceless shadows will drift over and spy on me. I'll be hunted down again, like a really tan and hairy rat. Not being able to look at yourself vexes your mind in unimaginable ways. I feel absent from my eyes, like I'm not really here, or the thoughts from my brain aren't truly going to my tongue.

How did they know?

I told Gerald about what happened, how I killed the thing by default, by its own mistimed stupidity. He told me to be proud. Regardless of luck the victory was mine. He was too afraid to fight these things, and he was happy I even tried to leave my hiding spot to seek vengeance. He said if I'm willing to march to the slaughter like a tiger, instead of lamb, then there might be hope for us after all.

I feel good. I watched the flawless blue sky and counted the breezes.

I feel good.

Day 48

We hid in the shed last night. I don't know why I wouldn't be in the house, it just didn't feel right. My uncle built the shed when my grandmother lived here about twenty years ago. It's a small tin box, with a padlock on the outside. The padlock happens to be my father's from when he was a kid years and years ago. Old, grey, and worn out—the lock helps with the appearance of sliding doors being clamped shut. The faceless ones don't know that the shut doors are simply an illusion. I haven't lost my mind enough to lock myself inside a shed.

Of course, my decision to stay inside the shed was completely impulsive and idiotic. I didn't even clean it out. Snowy and I just sat nested into the rusty wheelbarrow with some old propane tanks as pillows. Ling's family used to run the Hmong Soccer Tournament in Saint Paul every summer. They stored some tanks at my house while they were living in the apartment. They'll come in handy if it ever gets cold again, which I'm sure it won't.

You can't hide from anything; these monsters are proof of that.

They're built to find, hunt, and mutilate us to the finite degree. Talk about honesty, these beasts have it and eat it. Everything in this house has been warped by a fair amount of nostalgia. Now, it's just the plants watching, their canopies have a thousand eyes inspecting Snowy and me. She's not bothered by them, but I am, it's not natural, like I've said before.

Today, the heat curled my toes and made my sweat sink into my beard. It felt heavy and rotten. My head and face, felt like it'd fall off in this green cesspool of grass that's billowed against everything. Hot wind, stinky-sweet pollen, and an always sweaty forehead, that's our bizarre life now. Something has been lifted off of me since last night, since I tangled with that monster in my basement. I'm ready, with or without Gerald's help, to go out into the beating night. To make what happened in the basement a permanent excursion and pleasure. I forgot how brave you can be when met with the most deviled form of survival imaginable. I fought one in the truck and won. We explored the hospital through and through. I have killed one in my basement with nearly my own hands.

When my luck runs out, I'll probably die. Until then, bring the drum.

ILLUSIONS

Day 49

I was pretty gung-ho at the start of last night. After my battle with the faceless devil in my cluttered basement, I was pretty sure I could venture into the darkest and the drum, and not be humiliated or killed.

That confidence didn't last long. One night to be precise, or about eight hours give or take.

Last night, I took Snowy and waited outside my house where a couple of trees have toppled over in leafy bunches. They were sticky and sweet smelling in the heavy salt air. Both snowy and I started panting beneath the dull twinkles of the sun. We hid there until about seven, that's when the drum started.

It'd been a while since I'd been outside for when that slaughtering thunder starts.

I forgot how the air simmers and stirs right before the distant, empty smashes start. The shadows stretch, pulled by some phantom hands as unseen as the demons that stalk the edges. The dark shapes are contorted enough to snap, like some bizarre black elastic. The drum starts the moment the bands give way, like it's waiting for that quick leathery motion.

Snowy let out a little whimper the moment the drum started. I think she just wanted me to know she didn't approve of our little endeavor.

For the night, I had brought along my M16, my 22, a pistol, and four grenades. I wore my vest, along with boots, a pair of orange goggles, and some black gloves. I wrapped Snowy in this homemade sock of patched Kevlar. I was worried some sort of debris, or those poisonous thorns might hit her. My worry was well-founded I discovered.

They came out of the shadows—rising like curled pieces of cloths, then opening like spikey and shifting petals inside the sunlight. At least ten of them spawned around my house, including one just above me. It was one of those bigger monsters, with the dark-spore swept shoulders and red twisted skeleton. Its face, I wanted to see it, but it was hidden beneath the black cloud of shifting fibrous scales. I don't know why I'm so fascinated with them.

A few shots of gunfire hit the big one next to us. It immediately raised its mutilated arm up to deflect the bullets. The arm bubbled up like a row of fleshy flowers in blood. A man and woman, covered in dirt and blood were charging the monster. One of them threw something; it looked like a ball or something. I quickly curled over Snowy. Something exploded next to us. The monster absorbed the entire fire clap. A few pieces of debris ripped my ear, side, and knee. The beast's massive form teetered and tottered, I was worried it would fall right on top of us and crush us, or at least realize we're there and then kill us.

It was occupied luckily.

They shot it a few more times, before it charged. I didn't see what happened to the man and woman, but I know it crushed them quickly, in one long trail of pulpy flesh and blood. I heard the woman scream, but not the man. I don't understand why they

attacked it like that. I don't understand it all. The one night I
wanted to actually do something, these two idiots provoke one of the
big monsters in a moronic strategy. We crawled back inside the
house as soon as the full night came and the shadows stopped
meandering in the dusk. A few of the orange streetlights started
flickering on at the end of the block. I thought the power was all out
everywhere. It must've been some sort of glitch or old power
cycling through. That sounds wrong.

At least tonight taught me not to fight these things head on.
Also, that I had been one of the luckiest men on earth.

Day 50

I always knew things were beyond me. Last night, that belief was cemented, sculptured and verified. The one night, the one goddamn night I wander out with a small balloon of bravery holding my chest up and keeping the plant-swabbed fears from caving in, someone else decides to be brave and shows me just how easy it is to die.

I cleaned up the blood earlier today, it was hot and stinky.

I'm not sure educational would be the right word for what occurred. My father would use the line "enlightening," but that word doesn't remotely give justice to what happened last night. Those big monsters, the ones with those jagged, misshapen arms that expand, they're tough bitches. I'm not sure if I even have a weapon that'd be effective against their hulking forms. Grenades didn't faze them, so theoretically, nothing will? Doesn't really matter though, for the next week I'll strategize another route to take when exploring the post drum world.

We live in that world now, a pre-drum and post-drum world.

Talk about making me sick to my stomach. I'll take the gore and dried blood over our entire existence completely changing in just two months.

Really, that's all it's been since the first drum and the vague demons? During the day, like now, when I'm writing in this haggard notepad beneath a pair of overgrown tree shadows, it feels like no time has passed, not a single day. At night, in the dust and grime of hiding, where the faceless ones stalk every corner clean, those moments are equal to the millennia.

Talked to Gerald today, he spouted the same paranoia, same negative thoughts about the direction of our species. Sometimes, I wonder what he would have been like before the drum, before everything else. Would I still have talked to him? Was he this paranoid before, and the beasts just dragged it out of him. If they weren't trying to kill him physically, they certainly were eroding his mind and self-confidence. He might be right about the world being shit, but staggering around in the heat, mumbling about the plants and blossoms; it wasn't doing him any good.

I wish I could tell him these things. I wish I could tell him to keep his chin up and to stop acting crazy. My passive-aggressive side just hasn't quite run its course, even with this plant-wild apocalypse.

I'd better start getting ready for the drum.

Day 51

Snowy and I watched the trees today. I'm still a little shook-up from the other night still. I can't hide forever; the world's moving and changing. It might be easier to go outside if I didn't have Snowy, if I wasn't worried about her getting hurt. The monsters have absolutely no interest in dogs or animals. Like I've said before concerning the devils disinterest—I'm jealous. It might be safer for her without me, but Snowy wasn't raised to be independent and scour for food and water like a stray.

She's always been a dependent little wiener dog, and I hope she never changes.

Besides the few eviscerated people who I encountered a few nights ago when venturing outside, not a single refugee has passed through the neighborhood in weeks. I imagine the majority of survivors have stopped themselves from leaving areas of safety. If it's working—why mess with success? I wonder if any of my family still breathes and walks. The questioning feels like a muscle pain, it aches slowly and distant, but occasionally slips through in elaborate throbs. My family always flashes before my eyes the moment I wake up.

Always in the mornings, they're always in the mornings.

I've never written this much, or this consistently in all my life. I feel like I'm always repeating myself, but the days scarcely change without the drum. Plants blooming and wrapping the world in a sick pastel green. Cotton Willow seeds playing the hot air in idle drops and clusters. Cicadas are constantly buzzing arrogantly in the heavy eves, unchallenged by beeping car horns or trailing plane engines. The repetition of my journals syncs with the daily sun and moisture. I can't help but settle onto these images.

They're all I ever see.

I've started to read Hard Times by Charles Dickens. It was in a pile of old college lit books, which had been tipped off the bookshelf by the monsters. We really need to think of a name for them, something fitting. Anyways, the book feels poorly lit, dark, and ripe with economic toil, a concept distant from me now. Living, surviving, walking day-to-day, these are the true current problems. Hard Times feels like nothing in comparison to the drum and the faceless ones. Apparently, Laissez-faire capitalism was a driving thematic force inside the book according to the intro. I remember reading about it, but for the life of me, I can't remember what it actually might be. It can't be a very fair system of economics, or else Charles Dickens wouldn't write about it, that much I'm certain.

Snowy and I have acquired a favorite spot to sit in the hot afternoons. Right in front of my house, ever since my grandmother lived here, a birch tree has endlessly molted its paper skin. It's not doing that now; green vines have laced its crumpled shell tight. Still, the shade feels good, and the ground's soft at its white roots. I can usually read a few sentences before worrying about the night and thinking about my family.

When I first started reading it, it was only a few words.

I'll need to start scrounging for resources soon, or set up a system to capture water. The plumbing finally stopped, and I filled up as much water as I could in storage jugs, and hid them throughout my house. Only one rain storm in the last fifty days— just another frightening thought to add to my growing inventory.

I'm all stocked up these days.

Day 52

Last night, during the restless drum, I wanted to count how many times something scrapped against the shed, and crawled along the walls of my smashed in house. The shed doesn't have any real protection from anything, but I've had too many encounters at the house for me to feel comfortable there. The shed isn't too tedious, just a bunch of beetles and centipedes meandering their way in from the grassy edges between the silver metal and ground. I stuffed blankets there and sprayed some insecticide I stole from the house next door. It didn't really help—a centipede still ran across my face like a third eyebrow.

Today, I emptied the entire shed of all its tools and stuffed them inside the hollow walls of the basement. It was a noisy procedure, and a few of the increments jostled backwards as I carried them, hitting me in the face. It's been a while since I've sworn to myself. Spades, rakes, and other garden tools I never bothered to acquaint myself with, now have a permanent home in my basement. I feel like I'm burying a piece of the past or something, even though I never used these tools—but my girlfriend did. She had a lush garden just opposite of the shed in our backyard. It's been overgrown by lines of vines and ivory colored flowers.

On every surface the sun hits, flowers are blooming in strange patterns and colors, like an endless jewelry box was sprinkled empty on top of them.

More oven-air and hot breezes today, I'm not sure it'll ever change. I keep on mentioning it like it should change, but it never does. If things stay this consistent during the days, I'm going to have to start exploring houses again with or without Gerald. His behaviors have been a little erratic recently; basically, he's been talking to himself and staggering around the green-painted roads. We should be stocking up on food and water from other houses, and I want to ask him about it, but his eyes look so yellow now, and his lips are always dry.

When I was a kid, my parents always had this massive medical dictionary, which was a sky blue color with giant red letters. Whenever that book made an appearance on the kitchen table, like an ugly blemish, I knew something was wrong with them. I wish I had that book now, no matter how much it terrified me, just to look up information on Gerald. I wonder if it's dehydration or malnutrition. He's slightly older, but it's been less than two months since the drum started. Can it happen that fast? I'm not sure he'll ever adjust to this green land. I think he was having a hard time with the modern world already. I'm pretty sure he doesn't even have a converter box for his television. Not that it matters now.

I've saved the battery on both my IPod and laptop for when my mind truly gets desperate for a piece of the old world. I've huddled all my old pictures and favorite books inside the shed. I swept the brick floor out and threw blankets down with pillows and chairs. I made a cozy little bed for Snowy out of my old clothes, and rigged the door not to open from the outside with some wide chains

I found in someone's garage across the alley. I feel slightly bad pillaging and rummaging through people's stuff, but the situation isn't necessarily ideal for manners.

Tonight, for the drum, I'll watch the hammering darkness from my tin box. I've been watching the shadows from a vertical-scrapped peephole in the wall facing my house. I'll have to limit my gawking. I feel like the whites of my eyes shine so fearfully in the haze, that the monsters could pick them up blocks away.

I guess Gerald isn't the only one feeling paranoid.

Day 53

Last night, between the echoes of the drum, two fast moving jets roared over the neighborhood in diesel fueled howls. I loved the sound. I even counted its aching burst as it trailed away into my houses ceiling. People are still alive out there. Pilots are still flying the sky in the beast-soaked darkness. When the drum first started, I found some torn up wreckage of passenger planes closer to the highways. They'd been clawed to pieces like soft bread, so I'm surprised anything would fly, especially when the drum sounds.

It might just be an anomaly, I'll take it as a little hope, and a little optimism I can sink my yellow teeth into.

I finished Hard Times this morning. I liked the book, though, even in this sunlit and plant-forged cage, I could still feel that bleak British darkness. I wonder how Dickens would feel about the drum. Would he dive into it like he did the Industrial Revolution? I would hope so, faceless monsters trump economic development any day. But then again, I'm sort of a realist, but then again so was Dickens.

Leaving that sentence so open ended, I can feel an old literature professor turning over in his grave.

Gerald didn't come outside his house today. I felt weird walking up to his vine wrapped house and knocking on his partially smashed in door, so I didn't bother. You can still see blips of blue paint between the leathery tendrils and ivy. You would think the drum world would eliminate all these cultural considerations, like me leaving Gerald alone. Maybe if one more day passes without his shriveled form walking around, I'll go talk to him. I'm worried he's malnourished and dehydrated, but he's too afraid to ask for help.

I'm his friend, he can ask for help.

I explored two houses today. They were two brick ramblers on the outside of my neighborhood, closer to Golden Valley. Their doors were broken down and one was missing a portion of their roof. It looked like a toy house with a missing part; everything looks more and more adolescent with all this wanton destruction.

The first house hadn't been touched since the first night. There were trails of dried blood, but no bodies or pulp. The house had been torn apart by them as the searched it, but they'd clearly found nothing. The ivy inside the house was littered with blue and red flowers, gleaming like Crayola teardrops. There was a grey dust on their paper petals, like nothing had stepped in there for days. I avoided the mirrors in the bathroom and bedroom. They can't know I'm still rooting around. I found a bunch of canned food and a few bottles of water and soda inside the cabinets. I didn't stay very long, Snowy started to whine hysterically the moment we walked inside. When we left, I thought I saw something moving in the small slit of basement window.

Another monster locked away outside of night?

The second house had already been ransacked, but I still found a few cans and bottles of water. I wonder who pillaged it first. I hadn't noticed anyone except Gerald for weeks now. I wonder if it was the people who shot at us near Rainbow. Groups could be starting, militias or gangs. More questions, no statements or *answers to them. In the second house, inside the bedroom, there was a mirror on the ceiling. I didn't even realize it when I walked inside. I looked at it just for a second. There were no monsters, only a velvet black stretch of night sky, with small dew drops of stars glowing quietly. It looked serenely quiet, therefore hypnotically peaceful. I'd forgotten what it looked like.*

The bed beneath the mirror was bloody and sprinkled with befuddled feathers.

That brought me back to earth.

Day 54

Last night was another stale and stifling darkness in my shed. The drum boomed like always, the vine-tense thunder. I wonder if the plants make the sound, like some far away leaf-skinned snare drum. Something has to be doing it, some unseen and unknown horror. I'm sure the monsters have some tricks up their sleeves, or a new hand to be dealt. Sometimes, I dream about new shadows and shapes stalking midnight. I'm angry the fear has spread to my dreams, but it's easy to be paranoid when hiding in a shed every single night.

Today, I finally approached Gerald around noon. I knocked on his door, and yelled through the vine wriggled windows. Nothing, there wasn't a single shadow of movement inside his tiny, round house. I went inside after a few knocks, the place was empty, just streaks of ivy and dots of bold-colored flowers. There were empty cans and bottles everywhere. He'd been eating canned goods, and drinking bottled water. Judging by their clattering piles beneath my feet, he wasn't malnourished. I check everywhere inside his house, every small door. I announced myself enough times to cough in some of the pollen and dust weighing down the sunbeams. Nothing, there wasn't a single ache from his grey kitchen floors, his picture-cluttered walls, or the basement stairs where he'd hide during the night. Where would he have gone in the middle of the day? There were no signs the monsters had been there, no chipped blood or miscellaneous piles of dried-dark muscle. Why would he leave his house?

I did a once over across the neighborhood looking for Gerald. Snowy stayed next to my legs as we walked down each plant swept road. The hot air howled around us. It sort of felt like having all your windows down when driving down the freeway. The din blocked out everything around us, which was unsafe, because I couldn't possibly hear if someone was going to ambush us. There were possibly stray dogs too, since the monsters spare them, who were probably starving. I'm worried they might make a run at Snowy out of desperation.

I don't want to shot them. They're just hungry.

After a few hours, I stopped looking and went back to my house to sit outside on my wild front lawn. Where could he have gone? He had no supplies or nothing of value. The idea of marauders, especially after being shot at by those assholes at Rainbow Foods, isn't too farfetched. Why would they take Gerald though? Surely they would realize he's going slightly crazy and any sort of kidnapping wouldn't be worth it? Maybe he just wandered off somewhere.

I hope he's okay. I know I haven't spoken to him for a small while, but I miss him already.

The neighborhood feels even quieter without him.

Day 55

More drumming, more thick-dark nights, more clouds of dust and pollen waiting outside the shed door every morning when I rattle it open to the daylight. Every morning it blinds me, throwing round orange blobs on the outside of my vision, which dances away after a few irritated seconds. I need sunglasses, but when I wear them I hear my girlfriends chirping voice about looking like a stoner, or "like I'm too cool for school." I loved how corny her humor was—it was straight from the heart, without a lot of thought.

I've just realized, having paged through previous entries of my diaries, I've never bothered to explain why my dog has the title "Snowy," even though she's a small brown dachshund. My favorite comic growing up was The Adventures of Tintin by Hergé. I always wanted a little dog that could bite the ankle of a ruffian, or unlock a prison door with a paw. Now I have her, but this world makes those adventures look like a hazy dream that brews at early morning. Tintin never had to worry about the night, about the monsters coming, and even if he did—he'd figure out how to get rid of them.

How could anyone with such a ridiculous Cow-Lick haircut take on villainy with such ease? How would he do looking like me, a homeless-looking surfer with a random bald spot? Did the Cow Lick give him confidence?

I really need to shave my face. I just don't want to spare the water to do it. I might have to though; the itchiness burns up my cheeks to my nose. I wish the modern vanities would vanish from my personality, but I guess the whole word was running on it until the drum, so it probably has some staying power.

No sign of Gerald in our plant-wriggled neighborhood. I have absolutely no idea where he could be, or where he might've wandered off to. I scavenged a little bit further out into the plant-full houses. The vines wrapped everywhere in long green strands and sheets of ivy. They're inside houses, outside them; they're even in-between the walls in vein-like highways. What's feeding them? It's rained only once since the drum began. I've set containers out in random spots around my house. I'm hoping the monsters don't notice. When things first started with the drum and the dark, they'd come inside my house looking for the slightest hint of life. Even with my recent run-ins with them, they haven't done bothered with their search and destroy missions.

What's coming?

I can feel something running behind the hot air, something hidden but enraged. The flowers are everywhere, yet, they don't smell like anything no matter how many times I stick my face in them. I wasn't much of a flower connoisseur, but don't flowers typically smell like something. I wish I had some sort of book on the plant kingdom.

Hmmm... I'm not sure those words are correct.

Genus? That sounds more accurate, I wish had bothered with biology class a little bit more. I remember the book being giant and unwieldy. Life is apparently complex, yet it still flows by everyday like an easy string of water.

Tomorrow, I'm going to explore outside the neighborhood looking for Gerald. We'll walk all the way down to the Rainbow and the lake next to it. I might grab some water to shave. The lake water can't be all that polluted now, there are no boats, no people. I wish I could remember the name of the lake.

Tonight, before I sneaked into my shed to write, I noticed a few lights on at a house just down the block. The majority of the houses are completely swept up with vines, so not even their siding or decks glow through. Through their wild skin, I know I saw a few lights, and there were people around them. I watched their silhouettes. They were cutting a cake and blowing out candles behind a dining room window. I know I saw it.

I heard their laughter.

Day 56

Today, Snowy and I walked out from our neighborhood and its quiet, velvet houses. We walked past the Rainbow Foods, and onto the sidewalks near the lake. A brown sign, completely crisscrossed with vines, had the name of the lake, which was "Crystal Lake." I'm glad I know the name. Not knowing the name of any of the places around me makes this new world feel even more foreign to me. Why don't I know anything?

Was I always in such an unobservant cocoon rocketing back and forth through these stoplights and stop signs?

The buildings outside my neighborhood have also been sucked up by the green vacuum. Luckily, they're bigger and more rounded, the thin vines and trembling ivy have a harder time conquering the lengthy concrete. It's nice to see these businesses, and their names peering through the rising jungle. Wally's Carpet Cleaners, The Terrace Theater, Dots, and the New Shanghai Bistro all gleam along the brown strip mall attached to Rainbow Foods. The glass outside each store has been shattered and crumpled down by green-lumped hills of vines. It looks like someone looted Dots, judging by the trails of weathered clothes outside its doors.

A strange compulsion for fashion in this new and apocalyptic setting.

I was worried there'd be more stray dogs bumbling about these untraveled roads. I've rigged up an extended leash on my belt, just below my Kevlar vest. Snowy can roam exactly fifteen feet in any direction. Before, I'd let her off the leash, but since we're *exploring new territory, I don't want her distracted or vulnerable. I carried my M16 with me, and on my back I strapped my sawed-off 22 Gauge from before. I cut the barrel down to a shorter stub, since I noticed the last time I battled with one of these faceless monsters, the shotgun gave me suitable distance between their claws and gripping blades.*

If the thorns don't get you first on the small ones, or that extended claw of the big ones, they'll come in close for the kill.

Crystal Lake, what a lovely name, and it's befitting the appearance.

Whenever I would drive by the water on 81, it would simmer cloudy and dank, with a slightly pink chemical tint hanging on its surface, like a rebellious blob. Now the lake has a clear edge and center to it, like I can see completely into it from any angle of the forested shore. The plants have invaded the lake—from the banks on down, in leafy pipes and veins of green. They're clearing the water out, making it more inhabitable.

I filled a couple of gallon jugs with water, and tied them to the bottom of my backpack. The extra weight feels annoying, but it's not unbearable. I need the water to shave my face. If I had to drink the lake water, I would, but my supplies are still strong and hidden in canned goods and bottled water. My appetite has become based on energy and not taste, its consumption and not quality.

At the center of the lake, or at least further out from where I am on the shore, I noticed a strange formation beneath the water. It looked like someone had cut a bubble in half, and that perfect rounded piece and been glued to the green-heavy depths. There are carvings along it, strange twists of clawed figures and fire. In the center of the half-orb curls a rounded break like a sideways lip. I wonder if it opens.

I know it has to be related to the drum and the beasts.

On my way back home I walked behind Rainbow Foods. I figured if there were people still hiding there I'd either see them, or they'd see me. A hill crawls up behind the building. I walked up it slowly, trying to peer in the sandbagged entrance of the grocery store. Nothing moved, only a few scraps of plastic hanging off the rounded sandbags. There was a smell blooming out from the entrance—a stale and salty smell of oxidizing food. Nothing could be living in there around that reek; it made your eyes tear up from just a few hundred feet away.

I wonder if the monsters found them, or if they got in a firefight with some other irritable survivors. I memorized the pattern of sandbags and vines around the stores sliding doors. I'll check it out in few days, and if nothing else moves outside of it, I'll explore it.

On our walk back home, there were some wall clouds on the blue-blank horizon. Rain, let it please be rain.

The heat and plants have complete and utter dominion.

Day 57

Last night, behind the drum and all the hidden beasts, I heard a car driving around the neighborhood. Strangely enough, the acceleration was constant and uninterrupted. In the past, when I've eavesdropped on the nightmares, any vehicle brave enough to travel the darkness gets thrashed immediately upon its discovery. A few times, cars have only gotten past their motors ignition before screams and scrapping claws silence their engines. I would never be stupid enough to drive around while the drum beats. The car last night though, it kept on driving without being bothered by them. I even heard a slight melody of music inside the drum and engine. It sounded like Mozart, or Beethoven, or someone important to classical music.

I finally shaved this morning, and it was a very painful experience. I had some spare razors to take off the stubble, and I had my scissors to cut off the larger strands on my chin. Shaving without a mirror was the challenging part. I tried to use a shard of broken bathroom mirror for a few minutes, but the reflection became clouded with those grey figures from before. Eventually, the shiny piece was thick with them, and I was better off shaving blind. I made sure to expose myself to the reflection a block away from the house, just in case they employed search and destroy tactics like my previous experiences.

I'm not sure how many times I scratched my face, but it certainly hurt a lot. I'm worried about disease and open wounds with this humid and pollen-heavy air. I'm also concerned about the lake water I used for shaving, but I can only be afraid of so many things. It's a blessing in disguise that the monsters never left any full bodies for when the slaughter ardently occurred at the beginning. The streets would be swimming with disease. After I finished shaving, I dosed my face in after-shave and then sterilizer. I cried a little bit from it. I'll have to shave more often to get my skin use to the sensation. Snowy licked my face a few times after I recovered. The salt from her tongue stung my face, but I didn't care.

It feels good to have her concerned about me.

Yesterday, when I walked home, there were angry lines of storms on the horizon. They vanished overnight, like some invisible hand shook them into feathery dust. We need the water. We need a break from the stinking sun and breathing plants. I've got supplies, oodles of them to quote a serial killer, but paranoia still creeps into my thoughts about us running out.

I should start a paranoia list; Gerald, Snowy, supplies, the Drum, monsters, stray dogs, reflections, and possible marauders. Actually, looking at the collection of horrors doesn't make me too depressed. It makes me feel strangely organized.

Today, we walked back to Rainbow foods. It looked like nothing had moved on the inside of the entrance. I threw half-a-dozen small bottles of water inside the entrance. I left a small amount of dyed water inside the bottoms, so if someone moves them, they'll leave a trail. If someone walks through those shattered sliding doors, the bottles should move around. I'll have hard time distinguishing the dye from the plants and their rampant flowers, but I'll worry when it happens.

I want to go inside the building and explore, despite the sour smell of rotted food. I'm a little concerned about the darkness and being able to see inside the building. There could be stray dogs, or even a few monsters lurking inside the aisled shadows like when we explored the hospital. I found some flares during one of my mindless staggers, so I could try throwing a few in there for light. I have a flare gun too, which would be more fun and probably safer.

I've started to read The Hobbit by J.R.R Tolkien. I'm enjoying the book so far. I'm sure in all actuality, Tolkien would never have had the guile to take the trip like Bilbo did, or jump all over an adventure. Writing this sweeping fantasy epic might been difficult, but it pales in comparison to what I'm going through. I'd take a dragon, goblins, and trolls over the nightly drum and unidentifiable devils.

Why did our culture trivialize hardship? Why did we think this would be fun?

I wonder what strange things will be out wandering the night. I'm pretty sure I was dreaming when I noticed the family from a few nights ago.

The car from last night was real. I know it was.

Day 58

Last night, the lights and sounds came whirling down the street just like the monsters and their drum. Something's happening with all these pieces of the old world popping up at nightfall, I'm just not sure what. Last night, the drum was beating soundly, and I'm sure if I stepped out of my shed for one moment I'd attract one of them and be pulverized to a meaty pulp—and the world wouldn't stop spinning. It felt like the world had been petrified these last fifty days; specifically, with all the eerie consistency from day to night. Now things flicker and move in the steaming deep of night.

On the alley behind my shed, and the street in front of my house, streetlights flickered to life once the drum started in pollen-heavy orange glows. All of them glowed like clenched fireflies. A few jets buzzed slothfully overhead with a metallic slog, obviously unconcerned and unworried about whatever wandering monster made them crash when the drum began. A few cars buzzed by in trailed yellow lights and measured bursts of exhaust. I heard laughing out in the darkness, and delicate little voices.

I put Snowy up to the shed wall next to my spying hole for her reaction to all the sounds and sights. She twitched and shook her tiny tail at them, like she had missed all the random sounds of civilization. I wanted to go out into the sounds. They pulled out a thousand memories from my inner mind, everything from driving home on summer nights, to late night baseball games.

I couldn't stand the nostalgia and the sounds. I eventually plugged my ears with a pair of headphones and held Snowy against

131

my chest. I vomited once into a plastic watering can, mainly from all the headlights pushing between the thin metal walls. Why can't things have a semblance of natural normality? I know it's not right. I know the world wasn't coming back to life from this green prison.

Once the morning came, and the drum healed silent like a nightmarish migraine, all the lights and sweet sounds drifted away in the silver gloominess of sunrise. Clearly, the sounds and sights are related to the monsters, but I don't know why and to what end.

Moreover, I don't want to test this theory.

I spent the morning moving more supplies into the shed. I removed some of the tan, flat bricks to dig a hole to store the rest of my supplies. I lined the hole with tarp to keep them clean and free of bugs. I covered the hole with a variety of clutter to prevent marauders from pillaging my shed. I haven't seen anyone for days, but being shot at from empty spaces at a deserted grocery store makes you a bit paranoid. Ivy and green tendrils have washed into my house like living Halloween decorations. Pretty soon my house will be another green shell, hallow and vacant like a timbered skull. I hate it.

Today was a success though; I returned to the Rainbow foods to see if anyone or anything had disturbed my peculiar trap of food-dye-filled water bottles. They were still in their weird little pile outside the sandbagged entrance. We didn't require any more convincing.

The lights were all off inside the store, including the exit lights, which I hoped would be radiant forever despite the apocalypse. *It was weird to see the word "exit" dark. The air was sour with rotten food, even though the majority of the produce section was empty. A few fruits, mainly oranges and bananas, had rotted into a shriveling and unified mass, and had soaked the floor with their rancid, sticky juices. I kept snowy clung to my left side and M16 attached to my right hip. I was impressed I could carry the heavy weapon so casually, why couldn't I have been in this shape when the real world still existed?*

I did a quick walk of the entire store. I didn't want any surprises in the form of stray dogs or trapped monsters. Nothing moved, not a single shadow darted away under the trembling white egg my flashlight threw in front of me. Most of the shelves had been emptied, ripped apart or tipped over. I managed to find a few armfuls of random canned goods and boxed food, which I stuffed into my backpack and a duffel bag I'd brought along. I found some bottled water too, beneath a smashed shelf with dried blood on its splintered edges. Whoever was protecting this store clearly had failed, and these smashed shelves were a grizzly flag of defeat.

After I had grabbed my second armful of supplies, I heard a bizarre panting sound at the other end of the store. I heard a child crying and some steel-toed footsteps echoing upwards from the white tiles. I didn't want them to shoot me or Snowy out of fear. I also didn't want it to be one of those losers who'd been protecting the store from afar. I took us towards the back of the store away from the clanging feet. I found an exit door which led to the street and a steep hill. The moment I opened the door a quick beam of light blew into the store and for a second I remembered Rainbow for how it was before. I remembered taking my grandmother shopping their on Friday nights when she still lived over here.

Gunfire followed me in chambered-pops, and the white wall next to the exit door bubbled in quick holes of round brick. I ran up the hill behind the strip mall and hid next to an empty rambler just above the street. I waited and waited, until a thin, middle-aged man with two small children emerged through the exit door. They had a husky with them, and the father was pushing a shopping cart and balancing a rifle with his right hand. The children couldn't have been over ten and were covered in dirt. He too was dirty and scrawny looking. He had wild eyes. Even though they'd shot at me in the store, I was still happy to see them, and to see other people. I actually cried a little bit to myself out of happiness—as I ducked beneath the sight of his paranoid rifle.

He whistled at the husky to stay put, and I could tell it wanted to run up to us. I had to hold Snowy's muzzle shut to prevent her from barking. I hate doing that. I waited until they disappeared back into the store. I circled around the neighborhood twice on my way home, just to make sure they didn't follow us to my shed. I stopped a few times and spied on the green roads, which were thick with flowery air. It'd been hard to follow me with a couple of children.

I'm hoping to find out more about them tomorrow, maybe I'll stalk them for once. It was nice to see other people, even if the madness of this situation has made them a bit misanthropic.

Regardless, I'm going to read The Hobbit some more and hope for rain. At times, it seems like the sky itself has become afraid of them and their faceless shades.

Day 59

I've never been sure what actually happens when night falls. Since April and the lonely night at the bank, the drum has echoed, which brings them out to kill and mutilate us. It's now June, and now the nightmare has taken on new forms against the abdominal percussion. At least I think it's the darkness doing this, or them, the faceless ones. Two nights ago, street lights and cars beamed about the neighborhood's stale shadows. They looked, sounded, and even smelled real. I could taste their exhaust drift all the way into my plant shrouded shed. It was sour, smoky, and full of oil.

I never thought I'd miss the taste of pollution.

I know it can't be real. How could anybody think the world would just come back to life when the sun goes down? I won't lie. I won't deny how much I want to go out into the night, even with the drum and monsters. Seeing those fragments of the old world, of the pre-drum world, it clouds reality, and makes the night feel heavy and empty of symmetry like a deep dream.

I can't go out there and confront one of the images. The dark corners are bristling with them. I know it.

Last night, the images became even bolder. Lights turned on inside dark houses. Shadows moved back and forth in their windows. Husbands, wives, moms, dads, and children bustled through windows cooking and preparing, like the demons had never been let out of hell. Every light in the houses surrounding my shed glowed with the same absent orange as the streetlights did. I also noticed inside the rooms which were illuminated, the lines of invading plants were absent, like they'd never drilled their way through the siding or shattered windows.

The people in the rooms were fuzzy and without much detail, even with the lucid light. If they're playing with illusions, they need to refine their strategy, because they can't throw all these abominations at us and expect our forgiveness.

Still, I want to run out to them. I want to run to the windows and hot water. I want to see them, to commiserate with them, to weep about the darkness.

Old world images, but just clever pictures in a bleak portrait.

I wonder if this journal and all my ramblings will be part of a bigger picture someplace. If we survive the drum and all its monstrosities, I imagine there will be some history somewhere, and maybe my journals will be in some dusty hall with squared glass cases you can never touch; since they're protected by imaginary lasers.

On to things more pressing, like the father I ran into yesterday with his children and dog. I understand the situation our world has been gobbled up into, but I still can't justify his reaction to me. I'm sure he saw my form when I bolted through the exit doorway. The daylight blinded me as I ran through, and I'm sure I had an excellent silhouette for him to spy with his long rifle.

I feel like there aren't many people left anymore, even if we're all in hiding. Paranoia and madness seem like a couple of backburner problems, in-comparison to these unnamed monsters stalking us on nightly basis. The man shot at me without yelling a question or warning. His nozzle of gunfire did all the answering.

In his defense, I now feel more paranoid about my situation. Now I'm worried if Snowy and I wander too far away from my house he'll shoot us with his rifle, or his beast of a husky will rip my wrist apart and I'll die of an untreatable infection. These tongue-gnawing feelings still don't legitimize his hasty attack, but I do agree paranoia can be consuming.

Snowy and I stayed within a block radius of our house today. I walked down to Gerald's house to see if he'd returned. I yelled into his house in a more muffled tone, but still, just a silent doorway and plant-eaten walls answering my calls. I'm starting to wonder if Gerald wandered too far out one day, and this guy with his rifle shot him dead. The guy didn't seem explicably crazy when I watched him from a far yesterday, but it was concerning he hadn't bothered to bathe himself or his kids. After all, there happens to be a lake across the street from the grocery store. My freshly shaved face hasn't started to grow plants yet, so it then must be safe water.

Snowy and I are wearing our Kevlar vests at all times now. I didn't want to weigh down Snowy with this little Kevlar vest I made for her wiener-dog body, but with a husky, and possibly other stray dogs roaming about, the armor might be the only protection from their hungry jaws.

I guess I've always been paranoid about her safety, just not my own.

Today I read the Hobbit some more. It has been very distracting; therefore, I've been happier and it's been a supreme pleasure. Tolkien came up with such fabulous names for everything, and I can't figure out how he did it. Wargs, Gollum, all these great titles and names, which embody the characters and species they represent.

I wonder if anyone has thought of a name for our nightly demons. Could they really pick a fitting word for something we don't even understand, or have physically seen before? I think the monsters will always be the unnamed.

The Unnamed, yes, that has a certain ring to it.

THE

UNNAMED

Day 60

Last night, I wanted to go out to them. The images stayed the same; warm streetlights, the sounds of classical piano billowing out of open windows, and the random car motoring down the blackness. Tricks, they have to be tricks. I covered my eyes with an old yellow hand towel, and plugged my ears with headphones. The light was blocked well enough, but the sounds still bled through my headphones in distant melodies and roars. The drum mixed with the sounds in uneven, throaty intervals, like it understood the power of the old world songs. They're in correlation, they have to be. A living trick built by the Unnamed.

Yes, I like the ring to their name.

I noticed, before I blindfolded myself in the cramped darkness of the shed, no bugs buzzed around the streetlights or glowing windows. Legions of moths would ascend on a real light, especially with how insects have thrived under this new ecosystem. I hope other survivors notice this very important detail about the images, and ignore them. I'm not very smart; therefore, through deduction they should be able to figure it out.

Actually, I might've explained the logic wrong. I thought irony would disappear with television, but it apparently still exists.

I imagine there are loads of survivors in much worse shape than me, who might run out into the night dreaming of the pre-drum world. I'm still waiting for it to happen around me, to have some hiding survivor charge the lights. How will the monsters react? I haven't noticed them lurking in the booming shadows for days now.

I rearranged my shed, and concealed more of my supplies inside the ground. If marauders come looking for my food and water, they'll be forced to use their imagination to find it. Such a quality might be in short supply if you're malnourished and dehydrated. I ate a can of Ravioli today for lunch. I still have plenty of dog food and treats for Snowy, though I've rationed her down to two servings per day. The two armfuls of supplies I retrieved from Rainbow had a few boxes of dog treats. I'd feed her human food if I had to.

I sat inside my house for a while today finishing The Hobbit. I liked the ending, I read the Battle of Five Armies at least five times. I can't imagine writing such a pivotal scene with so many characters interacting. If they'd ever finished making the films, I imagine one entire movie would be this battle. I'm not sure what I'm going to read next, probably something lighter like Calvin and Hobbes. I remember reading them when I was younger and loving them. I keep the bookshelf in my old bedroom, inside the house, stocked full of books. A vine sits over the side of it, but otherwise it's been unscathed by the post-drum growth. I could take them out of there, and the Unnamed probably wouldn't notice, but the shelf wouldn't look right. I'd be lying if I didn't like a hint of normality in this green land.

I was actually sitting in my house, watching the street, when the husky came bouncing down the road in furry staggers. It was a pretty dog, colored dusty grey with blue-ice eyes, like they were chiseled for an artic shore. I wish I could say I was happy about its appearance, but I wasn't. I quickly put Snowy in my backpack, which I'd reinforced with patches of Kevlar. I didn't want her running around while bullets and bombs were smashing around. I ducked down on the vine -warped floor and watched the Husky stagger by in sweltering pants. The father and the two children walked slowly down the road behind it. One of the children stopped and peeked into a plant-heavy car with broken windows and a burnt dashboard. It'd been there since the first night. The father walked over to the child and soundly slapped him in the head. A patch of sweat flew off the child's face. The little boy immediately started crying. He couldn't have been older than eight.

I stepped out onto the street behind and clicked the safety off the M16. The husky immediately stopped and turned around with a growing growl.

"Don't move, and tell your dog to behave," I said. The father immediately froze along with the two children.

"You move at all with that rifle and you'll die. This is an assault weapon," I said. The man didn't move, his side was facing me.

"Why'd you shoot at me?" I said.

The man didn't say anything, he just stared at me with his rifle angled at the ground. He was covered in torn clothes and a shredded backpack. His face had some patterns of dried blood.

"Don't hurt him, he's deaf, and he's been protecting us for a while now. He doesn't know what to do anymore," the little boy gasped.

143

"Is he your father?"

"Yes, he's our dad, our mom's dead. They killed her on the first night."

"The Unnamed?" I asked, like it could be anything else.

"What?"

"Never mind, just keep moving through here. I don't want to hurt anyone or anything. Tell your dad not to do anything crazy."

The child spun a bunch of signs with his grimy hands. The father nodded and looked back at me with stone-serious eyes. He replied to his son, who walked over to me.

"He says we're walking to 100 to go south. There are more survivors there. We won't bother you again, just let us go." The child whimpered. I felt bad for him.

"That's fine, just keep walking. And watch out for images at night, I think they're traps by the Unnamed."

"The who?" the little girl suddenly said.

"The monsters, I've named them."

Snowy barked suddenly. I shook my waist a little bit to get her to calm down.

"A wiener dog?" the girl beamed.

The father hissed slightly and glared at her. He motioned with his head forward. The son had already started walking.

"Okay, well good luck," she said waving at me as they started off.

"Oh, have you seen an old man walking around here?" I asked with a hint of desperation.

The little boy shook his head and grimaced back.

"We've seen only dead ones," he said.

It'd been my first bit of real conversation in days. It looks strange and wicked writing down the dialogue on paper. It wasn't too terrible though, and hearing the children's voices will make me smile for the next few weeks.

Day 61

Last night, I employed the same desensitizing strategy to avoid the raw sights and sounds of this new issue. A few key-heavy melodies floated into my headphones like a broken piano lesson. The drum still bloomed about the darkness, and my headphones didn't do anything to stifle the shadow thunder. I'll never get away from it.

Typically, I don't think too much about the drum and its consistency, it depresses me on a very basic and primeval level. Every single evening around seven I pray a little to myself, or at least I pray deep in my thoughts without admitting anything. I'm not much of a hand-folding, speaking my mind to the heavenly-body type of guy, but a few helpful questions with no answers seem appropriate for this type of situation.

Apocalyptic situation that is, to be specific and to the point.

I'm happy with the name I gave the monsters, even if it's soaked with irony. It's not easy inventing a title for an unknown race of monsters summoned by a nightly drum. I could call them phantoms or wraiths, based on their flowing appearance. But if the criteria happens to be their look, then I could call them spikes, claws, or faceless. The Unnamed fits the unknown, so I'll stick with it.

I hope those kids pass on the name to whatever survivors they find over by highway 100. I'm not sure if there are actually living and breathing people over there, but if a colony has grown in the midst of all these plants and monsters, then good.

The waving and strangling heat drifted off the plants this morning like a sea of sweet smoke. The whole world has been tethered in this green, this ivy, these lines of vines with small flowers spiking everywhere like little tears. Houses have been completely covered and invaded. Trees are in full bloom. The grass on the lawns has grown up to my knees. Snowy can barely walk through the long grass. Cotton-willow seeds fill the breeze and occasionally my mouth. It's annoying.

I was happy to see those people yesterday, despite the awkwardness of the situation. Those kids looked rough, dirty, and ready for death. I hope their father gets them to a safe place. There are still people in worse shape than me, and that's slightly comforting.

Does it make me wicked for being happy about their hardship? I wish someone could answer me.

Today, I explored Crystal Lake some more. I took some more of the water for washing and bathing. I pulled a red wagon with me I found in a deserted background next to a playground. I filled up some plastic containers I found in some houses. I'm going to try and build a fire tomorrow and boil the water. That should kill any bacteria inside of it. I'll drink a little bit, and see if it affects my system. I've got a bunch of bottles of water still, at least a few months' worth, but I'm terrified about running out of it with this heat. I stopped at the Rainbow too and rummaged in the darkness with my flashlight. I found some more cans, but no boxed food.

The lake was overgrown along the paths and shore with vines. There were a few public beaches along the black asphalt path we followed. The sand had been spared the vines; in fact, they crawled around it in their wormy paths. The water was clean and clear throughout the entire lake. The strange shape of the lipped-line in the center of the lake looked untouched and pure. I wonder if it moves when the drum does.

The majority of the walk was uneventful and quiet. I kept an eye and ear out for Gerald, but there were no signs of anything around the lake. The big, beautiful lake houses Ling and I would dream about were now empty sockets of green and broken glass. No shadows moved in their absent windows or shattered doors.

Wealth isn't the top monster anymore.

On our walk back, Snowy and I saw something rather disturbing. I'd seen it before. I'd run from it before. I'd fought it before. I'd killed it before.

It was the Unnamed.

The vine-wrapped path was going up a hill towards a park when we saw it. It looked like a walking cloud of dragging darkness, with no real shape or definition. It had a cloak of sorts, only it was a mixing blue, green, and black. It had the golden blades from before, dangling from its fluid sleeves. Gold horns pulled up from the faceless blackness beneath its hooded cloak. No feet touched the ground as the monster walked.

It was a foot-soldier, not the big type with the mutilated arm. It was out in middle of the day without the drum wandering. The cloak that disguised them so well in the darkness was disorienting in the daylight, like a shifting fog of undecided matter. I grabbed Snowy and crawled underneath a bench just downwind of it. I had my M16 with me, and I focused the black sight on the sharp-floating monster.

It passed by me without a second thought, like an antisocial storm. I could've killed it at such a long distance, but who knows how many more are lurking out there without the drum guiding them. The Unnamed vanished into a small patch of woods up by the street. The cluster couldn't have been more than twenty trees, and it vanished completely into them like a sealed-bark door.

I didn't wait around for anymore observations. I ran home pulling the water containers. I almost soiled myself when I saw it. It made me sick to my stomach to see it in the daylight.

Why can't the nightmares ever stay the same?

Day 62

Paranoia. I thought it was bad before, like some distant sting at the back of a partially dried scab. Seeing the Unnamed in the daylight ripped open the wound, and simultaneously threw some salt and lemon inside it.

Even with all the supplies I was carrying, I managed to run the entire way home in the heat and pollen. Snowy ran right next to me in a sustained gallop. She rested the entire afternoon. She doesn't sleep when she's had too much exercise, but rests on the cold floor of the shed and wags her tail in random intervals. She only falls asleep when I'm sitting around her, which is often. We're practically attached at the hip.

Last night didn't help with the intense feelings of danger waiting behind every bundle of plants and caved-in-house. The drum sounded before the sunset, and the streetlights beamed on in artificial glows. Cars drove by in curling headlights. Music chimed and glowed between warm windows and distant alleys. The night was shifting with dark and deadly-life; in fact it was far busier than the daylight could ever hope to be.

I knew it would happen eventually, and sure enough last night in the dark it did.

Some fools were lured out by the images; specifically, two men and one woman. They dashed out of a house in the back alley, which had been long covered with lines of plants and flowers. They charged towards one of the cars bustling through the darkness. I'm not sure how long they'd been living inside the house, how they looked like, or if they were just traveling through and had picked that particular spot to hide, but it gives me hope and fear to know people were just a stone's throw away from me in all this thundering darkness.

I lost sight of the three people when they charged towards the car. The vehicle was sitting on the street just outside of alley behind my house. They called for help, for them to stop the car; I could hear their little strangled voices between the bugs and drum. The lights of the car glowed between the edges of the homes bristled sides, which looked angry and vengeful with plants.

That's when I saw the first one.

A medium Unnamed, a foot-solider, ran down the alley like a living shadow with claws. Four more followed it in a tight pack, and they hardly broke a leaf as they moved. The lights powered down behind them as they ran, like they were too afraid to witness what was about to occur. A big Unnamed, the grinder type with the mutilated arm, charged by the shed nearly knocking the walls down. The shed walls trembled like paper as it sprinted. Snowy barked before I could grab her muzzle, but the monster was too concerned with the people to notice. They don't care about dogs typically, but I didn't want to them to investigate the sound.

The moment the Unnamed rushed towards the car, the headlights, which were reflecting in the stuffy darkness, went out and the music cut from the air.

"Spores, they're just spores," some man screamed.

Gunfire followed in quick bursts, like condensed fireworks. Bullets rattled by my shed and the broken tree next to it. I hugged Snowy to my chest and turned my back to the battle. I didn't want a sly bullet to come through the shed and hurt her. An explosion shook the air around us, a grenade or rocket launcher. Screams followed, along with hisses and roars. More bullet fire popped out. I was too afraid to turn around and watch the battle.

I heard some gurgling and splashing sounds, like water being thrown on pavement. It had to be blood, it could be nothing else. Metal clanked down on the pavement also, along with some meaty thuds. There were more gurgles and echoes of trickling liquid. After the wet sound, everything went back to the drum. There were no more cars or melodies. The streetlights went silent and dark. Nothing moved, except the Unnamed and their deceitful darkness.

Throughout today I stayed close to the shed. The Unnamed I saw yesterday in the daylight, looked lost and confused, but it'd probably still try to kill me. I'm not willing to find out. I'll always keep a weapon close at hand from now on. I lined the shed with Kevlar vests. I have plenty of them, especially after the failed counterattack. I checked for signs of the battle yesterday, and found bloody clothes and shattered weapons. The guns being destroyed happens to be new, the Unnamed never cared about weapons before. The crater from the explosion yesterday has already been filled up by ivy and lines of plants, like those people never existed nor fought.

Day 63

I didn't sleep last night, and I couldn't nap during the day. My feet hurt from standing and walking around. Snowy's been able to sleep just fine through the sun and moon, like nothing bothered her. Watching them die last night in the darkness, getting carved up like screaming wet sacks by the Unnamed, it was all a bit too much. It'd been a while since I'd watched them move around, sneak through the dark, and rip people apart like dried jerky.

Yesterday, after the grim night of blood and screams, I spent the entire day pacing around the shed. In the span of 24 hours I'd witnessed the Unnamed out in the daylight by the lake, and then three people I didn't even know, who were hiding a stone's throw away from me, being tricked then mutilated by the monsters. For so many weeks the blood and viciousness of the situation hadn't bothered me, because blood's been absent since my bout outside the house with the grenades and the grinder Unnamed.

The world scares me because it can look so safe, but it's stuffed full of a shredding darkness.

Today, I considered moving to a different house, with less flimsy walls and not so out in the open. But then I realized the shed wasn't very intimidating; therefore, the monsters probably don't care about it in their grand schemes. Not that I understand their methods or strategies, but I certainly didn't fall for their pretty little illusions.

Speaking of which, they were out again last night in full mirage and might.

Cars and their yellow trails bounced between the spore-filled darkness, like a welcoming golden-thread of the old world. More piano played between the windows and wind-rolled curtains of leaves. The streetlights plucked on again with some magical orange power. The halos of bleached light looked empty, yet inviting against all the blackness.

I studied the empty spots and shadows for the Unnamed, hoping they'd expose themselves and their methods of hiding, but the shapes didn't look any different. How could they blend so well with everything? I know the foot soldiers have their blotchy cloak about them, which shifts to any color they want, but those golden claws and horns are unmistakable. The big ones, the grinders, they have a red-skeleton beneath their blackness, and light reflects off its marrow. They aren't hard to miss if you know what you're looking for.

I didn't do much else today except watch a few clouds drift across the unchecked blue sky. I want to wait one week before I leave my yard, in case the wandering Unnamed wasn't some fluke or anomaly. I already feel claustrophobic from just staying in my yard, house, and shed. I read two Calvin and Hobbes books today; specifically, "Something Under the Bed is Drooling," and "It's a Magical World." I'm desperate for more of these books; they were so much fun to read. Not a sliver of the nightmare world around me snuck into my thoughts while reading them. The only wishful thinking the books inspired me to do, was find a magical cardboard box so I could travel back in time before the drum. If I could do that, I would get everyone I loved together and hide from the drum.

I'd make multiple trips if I had to, but I'd do it.

There are clouds bubbling up on the horizon like grey bits of flattened fire.

Please be rain, please.

Day 64

Another terrifying night in the drumming world. A storm hit last night, which I was thankful for, since I needed to collect the rainwater and store it. The thunder sneaked up like a blazing shadow, and pretty soon the walls of the shed were wailing against rainy winds. I thought the shed was going to come apart against the gales, and flutter into the darkness like a pair of metal wings.

Snowy and I would be left alone in the maelstrom, and she'd probably run off into the rain and we'd both be scared and alone. Luckily, this didn't happen, though it felt like it did with every howl and boom of thunder. Snowy shook uncontrollably from the dark and stormy rage.

I had to hold her tightly to my chest to get her to stop.

The storms lasted for nearly the entire night, and didn't stop until early morning when the sunlight was blue and barely alive. The thrashing was so intense, it was like all these plants had stopped the rain from coming, so all it's energy had been bottled up for one primal rage. Fog billowed off the layers of plants like an angry breath, and blocked out all the empty spaces between houses and trees. I didn't move when the fog was out, it was too thick and smoky, like a thousand giant spiders had spun an uneven web.

It could be a trick, a ruse of the daylight to hide the Unnamed in amongst the ground clouds. I watched the puffs for spikes and claws, but saw nothing but the same houses and alleyways I had always known. It wasn't until the very last edges of the fog faded to nothing, that I left my shed, which wasn't until noon.

During the day I collected my rainwater from the containers I had spread throughout the neighborhood. Most of them were bottles, and gallon jugs, and each were at least half full. I covered each container and buried them in shallow spots in my yard. I made sure not to leave any tracks or trails for the Unnamed to find in the night.

I only wandered out as far the containers, which were all within one block of my shed. Each day I'll go a little further into the neighborhood, in the effort to avoid the Unnamed. It must've been a fluke. In the nearly seventy days, I've never witnessed an Unnamed out in the sunlight.

I'm praying it's a fluke.

Snowy had some sort of allergic reaction when I let her out after the fog went away. Her ears and head became full of lumps and hives, and her eyes swelled up they looked like they were about to pop out of her forehead. I found some Benadryl with all my junk, and gave her a teaspoon of it. I hope that works. She threw up too, and is breathing hard in little shakes of her chest.

I've never been so helpless.

GERALD

Day 65

I spent all of last night giving Snowy teaspoons of Benadryl. Her ears look the worst from the allergic reaction, they're raw with red sores, which look like they could pop open from the slightest turn of her head. She slept through the night fine thanks to the tranquilizer agent within the medicine. I wish I knew how much to give her, and how often. You take for granted all this knowledge when you have no access to it.

The whole world was plugged in, then, wrenched apart by these monsters.

Being disconnected this long makes you feel like your mind has lost the natural assuming mechanism of someone else always having the answer to your questions. It would always be Wikipedia, or Google to answer all my puzzles. I'm not even sure where the library might be from here, but that's the only place holding any knowledge from the bygone modern era. When I get my bravery back after witnessing the Unnamed wandering during the day, I'll stagger through the city looking for the old and eclectic 80's style building. I'll carry home as many books as I can, within reason of course, and the majority of them will be on survival.

There weren't any illusions floating around the plant-scathed darkness of the drum last night. Just the drum, the distant nightly thunder of a monster-soaked world. The air was humid enough to lick a dry stamp, to quote Newman from Seinfeld. I wonder if the wet air stopped all the spores from floating around, just like the night before with all the heavy rain. The Unnamed have cloaks of spores, which mesh in darkness and camouflage them. The dead men, the ones who screamed the other night, they said the speeding car was only spores.

Clearly there must be a connection, but how does this synchronization become a weakness.

When the morning finally pulled the sun up and knocked the drum away, a surprise was waiting outside the ivy wrapped wall of my house. Gerald was back, in the flesh, and living. He was actually clean and washed, full-looking and less gaunt than when he wandered off weeks ago.

I couldn't believe how happy I was to see him, like I hadn't seen anyone I'd known since the drum started. Snowy, who has been bogged down with the Benadryl the entire morning, ran out for a belly-rub in the long grass. Gerald was happy to see us, and was carrying a bag of water and canned food.

He'd gone looking for his children, and went 10 miles in every direction hoping to run into survivors who might know them. He found a few clusters and colonies of people who had banded together to survive the nights. The biggest colony he found was in Brooklyn Park, and had over a thousand people living inside of it. Every night they'd find hiding spots and places, and looked out for one another with the Unnamed.

He said they nursed him back to health when he staggered into the camp. They'd basically saved his life. The place was called the Third Colony; apparently the first two had failed before this one. He decided to come back to Robbinsdale to find me and take me there. I couldn't help but hug the little old man and lift him off the ground. I was so tired of us being alone in the darkness.

Tomorrow, we'll walk to the camp during the day. He said they had networks set to find lost relatives. He didn't hear anything about his kids, but maybe I would hear something about my parents, Ling, or more.

I'm feeling so much better about the drum, the sprawling plants, the ridiculous heat, and the nighttime illusions. Even more amazing, when Gerald related this entire story to me outside my shed, he referred to the monsters as the Unnamed. Those kids listened to me, they lived and they spread my name for the monsters. Maybe someday the world will know who named these godforsaken beasts.

I can only hope.

Day 66

I'll start with last night -- when Gerald and I hid inside my shed during the drum. The illusions glowed out of their hiding holes, and the night air was filled with the sounds of music, cars, and everything else in-between. I even heard whistling in the darkness, granted, it was faceless and shadow-laden, but whistling nonetheless. Gerald hadn't been part of the dream-darkness yet. Luckily, he was in better spirits and health thanks to the colony, so he could grapple with the strange set of emotions befalling you upon witnessing the pre-drum world rise out of the plant-heavy deep.

I was a little worried when he first started watching the streetlights and the orange-filled window panes. The glow can hypnotize if you stare too long at it. I let him soak it in at first. In fact, he kept on mumbling, "This has to be real right? This has to be?"

"No Gerald, it's a trick, I've seen the monsters come out of the lights. They're all waiting outside for us," I'd whisper to him.

"I haven't heard music since the start of it all," he'd say.

"They're all spores Gerald, it's not really there," I'd say.

We'd repeat the same conversation over and over, until he accepted the illusion, the plant-painted portraits of our lost world. He cried a little bit in the darkness. I did too at the beginning of it all. It makes you doubt every little thing about yourself, like you're caught between two nightmares; the daily scavenging of a plant-ruled world, and the nightly drum of spore-clouded shadows. Trying to decide which world was more horrible was a waste of time, since each had their drawbacks, and flaws. The daylight might be worse, since you know the drum would be coming, like a long lost demon thrumming his thunderous wings in the deep night.

Gerald and I didn't sleep the entire night. I was too worried about him running out to the mirages, and he was too entranced by them. Eventually, dawn came in a yellow heaviness, and we staggered out of the shed with a renewed focus. I packed my backpack with food and water, and hid the rest of my supplies in the ground. I packed my M16, pistol, my sawed-off shotgun, and some grenades. I was worried we'd get caught out in the darkness. I put Snowy inside my backpack on top of the food and water. She's been doing a little bit better, but I can tell whatever she reacted to really took a lot out of her. She's been sleeping more often, and breathing very hard.

I can't think about it, it's too hard.

I've been hiding a bike inside the shed. I didn't take it out too often because I don't want someone to rob me for it, and also because the tendrils of ivy and vines have made riding on it unbearably painful. Today, I'm going to use it, since Gerald rode one back from the colony.

We rode for at least three hours, down 81 to Highway 100, where we took the old freeway down to Brooklyn boulevard. It was hard to see the world. Everything has been choked by green, like the plants are trying to squeeze the concrete out like a puss-stocked sore. Buildings, roads, light poles, stoplights, even benches all had *a velvet skin of leaf and vine wrapped around them. The roads are warped by their invasion, causing bumps and bruises with every passing second. We had to stop multiple times because the bumps were too hard. My ass and inner thighs feel raw and skinless against the seat. I've lost so much weight from my canned-food diet. It's mostly bone down there now.*

The colony was working out of an old shopping mall called Brookdale, which was right off Highway 100 North. We walked the last half of the trip since we had time to spare. If you ever want to travel in this new drum world, you need to leave plenty of time open for the daylight. I let Snowy walk with us towards the end of it. I hadn't noticed any dogs or anything dangerous roaming the concrete infused jungle.

Gerald was surprised and saddened the moment we exited the dilapidated freeway. Nobody greeted us. There were no signs of vehicles, or anything, just silence from the plant-warped shopping mall. Brookdale was just a tiny block of building, with a few wings of empty stores. Nothing moved outside of it, not a single shadow in the hot sun. The front of the wall was full of massive windows and doors, which had all been shattered. Gerald ran up to them and darted inside the mall. He said the windows weren't broken before, that the beasts had left it undisturbed.

Inside the long corridor of Brookdale, we found remnants of the thousands of people in bloody scraps and broken weapons. It was like someone had sprayed the ceramic ground in uneven shades of red, and held the nozzle down and let the paint pile onto itself in dried clumps. The entire inside of the mall was covered in these crimson, inky shapes. We only walked halfway in before the stench of rotting blood completely controlled the air. Shattered guns and bullet casings shined in the grim sunlight shooting through the malls windows. I grabbed some food and water from the bloody ground, but literally every single weapon from knife to M16 had been destroyed by the Unnamed.

Halfway into the mall, we found the cause of the attack. Someone had brought in a long-mirror. The monsters had noticed the colony through the reflection and stormed in during the night. If it had been at dusk, when the drum first starts, these people might have had a fighting chance. Gerald destroyed the mirror, shattering it with the butt of his rifle over and over again into dust. When he finally stopped panting above the crushed silver, he was sweating and crying.

He had hope. He had tasted it when he'd lived here. I had none to begin with, so I was somewhat okay.

Nonetheless, neither of us spoke the entire walk home.

Day 67

I wish I could think of one single thing to say to Gerald to help ease his mind about what's happened in the last twelve hours. The lack of socialization from this plant-monster haven, this Greenland world, has taken its toll on my social abilities.

In just one day, the entire colony was destroyed and hopelessness returned.

I just don't know what to say to Gerald.

In the span of two days, he'd found a colony with civilization blooming back up again, like a competitive flower in this warped-weedy world. So many plant analogies drifting through my mind when I write. It's driving me insane. They're everywhere and on everything, like a new skin on a wound. Only this new green scab isn't healing the blood and puss beneath it, but dominating it and altering it's composition. The world was ripped to pieces by the drum, and the plants are helping it.

Last night was sad and awkward. I wanted to tell Gerald in the thick air of my shed it was going to be okay, and more colonies would get established. My positive attitude probably sounded ridiculous, since I'm just as hopeless as Gerald. I'm shocked someone made the crucial mistake of bringing a mirror around so many people, knowing the Unnamed are lurking behind every reflection. When the drum first started, the reflections would cause the Unnamed to appear and search wherever you exposed yourself to the mirror. It wasn't hard to figure out, since the Unnamed always appeared in the reflection in foggy and faceless clouds.

What vain idiot would bring a mirror in? Hadn't they noticed this since the start of the drum? Hadn't they noticed they were in the middle of plant-monster apocalypse?

I shouldn't dwell on idiocy, it's just there isn't very many of us left, and when things like this happen, it reduces the small amount of hope you hold within your chest to a whimpering vapor. It makes you wish the Unnamed would rip this shed down and peel us apart in bloody sections of stringy sinew. Our bodies could be like string cheese to them? They're that intimidating. Is it possible to have negativity go negative? If so, it's happening right now in this shed.

The illusions were out last night in their warm edges and distant fogs. The drum boomed emphatically and solemn, like the jaw of a predator slowly closing around some shivering prey. Gerald cried all night long, like a lost child. It was loud, weepy, and full of groans. I was afraid he might attract the Unnamed, but what could I say to my friend? I was just glad he was back, and that there was someone for me to finally talk to. I stayed up all night watching him cry.

We almost had it, a piece of our old world again.

In the morning, Gerald moved a few of his things into the shed. Mainly his weapons, water, and leftover food. We have a bunch of it now, enough to last us a more than a few months. I'm glad he's willing to stay together through all these horrors. Snowy's really attached to him, it's almost like she was tired of me and all my wanderings. She's feeling better, but she still has a whole constellation of hives on her ears. I gave Gerald a few books to read to keep his mind off the drum coming in the evening. He didn't even pick them. He just listened to his little battery-powered radio. Nothing but static, not even the emergency sounds chime anymore in their melodic brags.

I told Gerald about the Unnamed out in the daylight, the one who wandered around like a spiked cloud in the sun. He didn't believe me. He actually laughed at me. I know what I saw, and I didn't take too kindly to be laughed at. I actually shouted at him about it. We're both frustrated by the loss of the colony. Regardless, I'm making Gerald go with me to the lake tomorrow to see if we can see it.

I need to know if we should be afraid during the day as well, or if it wasn't just one tiny occurrence. We biked all the way to Brooklyn Center yesterday and didn't see a single one.

Also, tomorrow we're going to kill the Unnamed if we see it. It's just one, and we have the weapons for it. We'll watch and shoot from a distance, and see what happens. They're too dangerous at close range.

They're too dangerous all together.

Day 68

Nothing ever goes according to plan.

I'll start again with last night. Not much actually changed from the other nights. More darkness, drums, and illusions. More giggling in the shadows, and strange music falling out of half-lit windows. More shapes gliding around rooms like enslaved silhouettes. More crying from Gerald, hushes by me, and whines out of Snowy. The humid air billowed between the thin shed walls, and the plants curled menacingly in the darkness.

All in all, it was a standard night with the drum.

In the morning, we immediately started walking towards Crystal Lake, which was the earlier site of the daylight Unnamed. We walked carefully and slowly, just in case the monster was waiting for us in some sort of bizarre ambush. I had witnessed their ambush at night at the hands of those illusions, but how the Unnamed would operate during the day was a complete mystery. When it staggered past me, it looked sick and anemic, like it wasn't truly there.

It's too hot and humid outside to carry extra gear with us, especially when we needed to conserve our strength for killing this Unnamed. Gerald had his rifle, and I had my shotgun and M16. It'd rained twice since the start of the drum, which means we should expect rainfall once a month. The unchanging humidity might be worse than the Unnamed in some respects, especially since we get a break from the monsters in the daylight.

We set up our sniper spot on top of a playground about two hundred yards away from the bench where I saw the Unnamed. The playground was completely covered in plants. We had to tear some of them apart to even find a place to kneel or sit down. Eventually, we made a spot on top of a round slide, between some narrow bars. Gerald set up his rifle just above the fencing. Snowy came with us also, I won't be leaving her alone during this allergic reaction.

We waited most the day in our little hiding spot. The sun burned us, and gnats constantly wandered over in angry little clouds to bite our eyes. We both wore Kevlar vests for protection, and the armor combined with the heat made us sweat in a thousand different places.

We each probably drank one gallon of water, Snowy included.

Around four o'clock we saw it. It walked, if you could call it that, down the same hills and paths from before. It followed the outline of the lake like an angry cloud. It looked the same as before, spiked, foggy, and strangely hooded with a dark and fluctuating cloak. It was heading for the same patch of trees as before. Gerald started shaking and gasping at the sight of it. He dropped the rifle and cowered back against the monkey bars.

I'd forgotten whether or not he'd actually seen the Unnamed before.

I picked up the rifle and followed the black sight down. It took a few seconds to get use to the perspective. The numbered grid eventually focused on the drifting monster and I pulled the trigger. The shot echoed across the Greenland world. The Unnamed shook for a second like a startled animal and turned toward me with its shadowy head.

It had found me that fast, I couldn't believe it.

It started to run towards us like a bladed dark-wind. I fired at it multiple times, but it jumped wildly like a cat back and forth, leaving small plums of dust behind its nimble body. I threw down the rifle and picked up my M16. In that small amount of time it'd closed the gap between us and was running for the slide. I fired a quick burst into it, which slowed it down for a second and knocked it off its feet. It crawled onto the slide in a hooded shutter. Thorns hit the playground around us. Gerald grabbed Snowy who was shaking and curled against the wall as the black points fell on us. I ran over to the top of the slide and fired into the Unnamed at point blank range. It hissed and shook like a trapped fog, but still crawled upwards.

My clip went empty as it reached the top of the blue slide.

Without even thinking, I kicked the monster in its shrouded and gold-caged chest. Thankfully, the Unnamed was weak from the gunfire and toppled back down the slide. Still, it was like kicking a living wall. I followed and fired five shells from my 20 gauge shot gun into its quivering mass. It went still with a quiet hiss, like steam being released from trap.

I ran down to the body to look at the monsters face. The hood was completely black, but moving, like a living darkness. At night it was always too impossible to see its face, since in the shadows they were more camouflaged. As I approached it, the plants, which had invaded the sandbox in a green carpet, clung onto the Unnamed like a sleeping child and cocooned the body in a slow wrap of ivy. I jumped back onto the playground, afraid the green tide might suck me in.

They really were working together.

Before the Unnamed was buried away, I saw a glimmer of its face. It was white, lined and soft, like layered petals. It had two eyes, but no mouth or nose. It was like a delicate pearl mask behind the spore-darkness.

It was strangely -- beautiful?

How could something so violent look so unblemished?

Day 69

Before I can talk about today and last night after our little skirmish with the Unnamed, I should elaborate about what occurred after we killed our daylight-walking fiend. The moment I slayed the confused and wandering Unnamed, the plants beneath its feet wrapped it wildly, and swept it away like a dead bird. I briefly saw its petaled face, a perfect mask carved by the drum and plants throughout this new world. It didn't look just like a monster, but something far more intricate and delicate, but still wild and dangerous.

The branches started to roar after the Unnamed's death, like a hurricane had been shackled between their leafy arms. The gust howled around us, circling the playground and vines, which chattered like a bunch of narrow green snakes trying to shake away their skins. We immediately jumped off the playground and ran towards home like a pack of irritated bees.

With relative ease, we dodged buildings, fallen trees, and burned out cars, like the entire army of invisible monsters was on our heels. The roaring sound of the leaves, it was like every eye the Unnamed had hidden in the daylight had suddenly turned and fixed them on us. During the sprint, I managed to yell to Gerald that we should zigzag our way back to the shed. Whatever phantom was following us, I didn't want it to find our nightly hiding place.

Gerald did one better with our run back -- we actually hid at his house a while before we sneaked back to my tiny shed. We waited inside his house until the breeze went quiet and returned to *its drifting glides. It took a full four hours for the world to calm down, like killing the Unnamed had disrupted the natural balance of things, and now the daylight was hunting us too, just like the nightly drum.*

Gerald and I talked about the feeling that made us run so frantically. We couldn't pinpoint the fear, but it felt like something horrible and surreal had just been wrenched out of the daylight.

Killing the Unnamed was against this new living order ruling our world. The sickness, the stinging-sweet smell of all the flowers shaking, and the roaring trees, it was pure rage.

So the night came like it always does, and the drum sounded right before eight in the waning orange beams of the sun. We waited in the shed with our gun's safeties off. Gerald wanted us to dig an escape tunnel through the bottom of the shed, so we'd have someplace to go in case the Unnamed realized our location. I'm too worried about the natural gas lines beneath our buildings to even contemplate a tunnel.

The night was stocked with a horde of Unnamed. They scoured every inch of my old house, backyard, and neighbor's houses. They crawled about on all fours like animals, like they were desperate and rabid to find our hiding spot. This strange vengeance fueled search, coupled with the fact they never leave their dead behind, makes me worried the Unnamed are so much more than just masked killing machines.

There were no illusions beaming about the darkness during their frenzied search. They cancelled them to look for us. How could

174

they cancel their mirages like an afternoon play performance? The synchronization between the plants, monsters, and illusions must be like a symphony of sorts, or completely in beat to make it all function.

There has to be a crack in their armor, but what?

We spent the entire night holding our breath. We stayed perfectly silent inside the shed, even Snowy didn't breathe loudly. We watched hundreds of the Unnamed drift by like living cloths of night. The trains of spiked clouds and red skeletons were endless. The sky came alive to twisting pieces of black fabric and white masks. They have monsters in the sky. They've always had monsters in the sky.

When morning finally arrived, and the daylight melted the shadows and Unnamed away like a steamy cloud of dew, Gerald and I started to hunt throughout the neighborhood for a new hiding place. After constantly second-guessing ourselves and finding every conceivable error with each basement we searched, we decided to stay in the shed. If they actually knew we were there, we'd been dead last night.

We spent the rest of the day sleeping, but with lingering paranoid thoughts of the plants growing larger, the drum louder, and the Unnamed becoming more and more human.

Day 70

They were thick last night. They practically blocked out the gloom and darkness with their spiked clouds. Gerald and I watched them all night. They trickled through my backyard like a demon-river, like a monster stocked pipe of restless devils.

Once again, we stayed up all night waiting for the Unnamed to bristle into our tin box. To shake us loose from these flimsy walls, and take us outside in flailing chunks of screaming meat. I can't help but think we're tuna inside this shed, waiting to be peeled out and torn to pieces by a thousand clawed arms of unknown monsters.

I hate thinking we're tuna, spam, or any other sodium preserved food.

What makes the analogy worse is the sweat pouring out of our skin at an alarming rate. We're literally being canned and preserved for the Unnamed to devour, like a long lost can of meat at the back of a cluttered pantry.

Writing this much about the same things over and over, everything is turning into a metaphor.

No illusions again last night. My killing of the Unnamed in the sunlight must have thrown off the delicate balance that makes this drum world work. The festering paranoia from the bout might not have been worth removing this creature from existence. It's very discouraging watching the monsters horde about these last few nights. They're mortal, and capable of being killed by our guns, bullets, and bombs. Why are there still so many of them roaming about the darkness? Even if those confrontations between the military and Unnamed failed, they still should have wiped out a bunch of these monsters. I don't understand why there are still so many?

Another downside of watching these monsters the last few nights has been the grim realization they're stalking the sky. I remember during the counterattack, I saw something tear a jet apart in the star-dotted blackness. These last few nights the sky has been writhing with whatever abomination throttled that plane. I can't get the best looks through the rust-lipped cracks of my shed's roof, but to me they look like pieces of flowing black cloth with white and flawless masks. The masks have faces on them. Those flying monsters aren't just some drifting masquerade.

After all, I saw one chase down a jet

We slept during the day, again. I do not like this type of routine. We have plenty of provisions and water, so gathering more isn't an issue. The feeling of profound hopelessness is a more pressing issue however, and it feels more powerful during the day. I couldn't even concentrate on "The Indispensable Calvin and Hobbes," and nothing has ever stopped me from reading them. How long until the legions of Unnamed brush up against our shed and one of us screams?

Gerald suggested we move today, but the whole area becomes thick with them, and staying in the heart of this monster-maelstrom might be the key. Survival out in the open, hiding in the open, someone I know was in a play called. My family, please let them be alive. I can't write about them, because then I'll start to think about them. I can't let everything get away from me.

I just can't.

Today, a roof on the little rambler across the street collapsed beneath the weight of the bristling and building plants. It shook the whole neighborhood in a booming and broken crash of rotted wood and hollow metal. The sound only happened for a second, as if the plants didn't want to bother anyone. Nothing moved when the house caved in, not a bird or bug. Gerald and I looked at each other when it happened, but we didn't say anything to one another.

The plants are going to get rid of us one way or another.

Day 71

I knew Gerald wouldn't be able to handle the nights for very long. The throngs have stopped storming through the backyard in those silent clouds of dangling claws and bristling spores. They went silent like an errant gust of plant-soaked wind, and echoed away into the dark spaces between our houses and nightmares.

I know they are out there though, sniveling away between the trees and plants like clawed cockroaches.

Last night, the illusions came back in full force and renewed power, like those monster artists had been locked away with eager quills. There were cars buzzing around. Lights flickered along the alleyways like lazy orange eyes. Bugs drifted past them in disoriented clouds. The light didn't look real on their petaled little wings and bodies, like one of those screens for movies where they draw everything in.

It was too much for Gerald. When he came back I knew it would be. I knew it.

The sounds, the old music playing about the lit windows in piano heavy lullabies, they pulled Gerald's eyes out of the shed and into the darkness. Tears came too, like guilty little swallows of salty water. Every single night they've come out, Gerald has been weeping to himself under the shed's roof. He kept putting his withered hand over his mouth and mumbling: "It's not possible, not possible, how can they still be there, how can they still be out there."

He was saying it too loud last night. It's been getting steadily worse. I actually considered knocking him unconscious in the stifling air. I held it in though, the rage, the rage that he can't see what's going on around us, and that his own fear could kill us. I know the Unnamed are watching us for the slightest error. I kept whispering to him to be quiet, but he kept talking to himself.

The night finally ended with the whistles of morning birds and glows of rising steam from the puddled plants. It looked serene and pretty absent the distant drum, but it always does. Gerald ran out of the shed the moment we opened the door. He said we needed to find a new place to hide, that he insisted on us changing our location. I get his fear, but they've got to be watching the whole area for us to slip up.

We argued all morning about it. Once again, I contemplated knocking him out so he could just calm down. Eventually, he stormed off down the block with his rifle over his shoulder. Snowy barked at him to come back, and I yelled and swore. I called him an old-stubborn-asshole. It was a little melodramatic, but he's the only human being I've really talked to and had in my life since this whole thing started.

And he's my friend.

I gave him a little space when he staggered away through the vine wrapped houses. A few more roofs collapsed in the distance as he walked away. They echoed like old crumbling gods giving way to some new order, but with prayers of aching wooden moans. And the world was giving way to the drum and its new ecology. After a

few hours, I went looking for him. I checked his house, the
neighborhood, and everywhere I could.

    He'll be slaughtered, they're looking for us.

    The drum is coming fast tonight, like it wants me wandering
out there to find Gerald. I don't know what to do.

Day 72

Gerald was a fool, and I cared for him, but he couldn't listen to me. I've killed and survived these beasts well enough for now, but he couldn't listen to me. He couldn't give me any credit or any dignity with the situation. It might've been because he was older, and supposedly wiser, but I don't really know. I know I say it all the time, but there are so few of us left in this green and warped world.

Now there is one less of us.

I stayed out on the plant-wriggled road until the very start of the drum. The sunlight had an orange skin to it, like it would peal apart in the dust and heat. The trees are so heavy with overgrown branches now. It makes the rays of light nearly vanish before they hit the ground. They have to take everything away, like our evening light, like our sun.

Typically, I don't like to wait outside the shed until the drum starts. The Unnamed appear so fast, they literally rise up like stifled corpses from the shadows. Then they rush and charge, scouring the edges and corners of homes before their illusions blossom from their vine-happy allies. I had to wait out there till the last possible second though, it was a must. I couldn't let Gerald think I'd vanished, or that I had just locked up the shed and wouldn't let him in.

The moment the drum started I sprinted to the shed and closed the door. I was lucky enough to dodge them, especially since the Unnamed had been spying on us so ardently the last four days. I thought they would've had sentries or spies watching my house the moment the monster-thunder started. The holes in their strategies can sometimes be surprising, since they live on mirrors in daylight, they run along roofs and walls, and they live through explosions and tank shells.

It just seems like they can do anything they want.

I waited inside my shed with the safety off my M16. I watched through a crack in the siding, spying on the darkness. The sun dropped down fast and deliberately, like it wanted to watch the night unfold as much as I did. Nothing moved for a while beneath the drums, and the illusions didn't stir much either. Only a few streetlights flickered on with artificial power, throwing their blotchy dull circles of light onto the dark pavement. Nothing moved for the longest time, not even the insects. I checked the edges of the houses for their sharp and cloudy shapes, but there was nothing.

Then I heard the rifle shots. They popped through the night like tin firecrackers, pushing their way into the ominous thumps of the drum. The smoke of their canisters echoed for a few minutes on the midnight air. Running soon followed, and I could hear someone panting wildly in the darkness, just outside the shed. Heavy and panicked feet smacked between the plants and concrete. I knew it was Gerald. I got my gun ready. I put Snowy in my backpack with the Kevlar so she wouldn't have to sprint after me once I got outside. I also didn't want any shrapnel to hit if I used a grenade. I was about to undo the chain from inside the shed and slide open the door when I heard a voice yelling.

"Don't get out of your hiding place don't do it," the voice said. I knew immediately by the huskiness of it that it was Gerald. He was yelling. He must've started running to the shed and stopped.

"The Unnamed are everywhere out here, they'll swarm you, don't you dare open that door," Gerald yelled with hidden-sobs starting.

I wanted to yell back. I wanted to say something, anything to make him feel better.

"They'll kill you if you speak, don't do anything, don't you dare," Gerald said, getting more control over his voice.

There was silence and drum echoing.

"They want to lure you out, they want to find you," Gerald said.

Something big brushed against the shed. I chewed my lip open with nervous bites.

"I'm sorry. I should've listened to you, don't be sad, you're not alone," he said.

I started to cry behind my tin walls. He was my friend. I didn't want him to die.

"They're coming towards me, it'll be over soon. Don't be afraid, you're not alone. I should've listened to you. I should've--" Gerald said. There was a crunching sound, followed by a splashing and faint gurgle. Something soggy thudded against the ground over and over again, and a metal-hungry scrapping filled the blackness.

They were tearing him apart, I knew it.

In the morning, I found his body mostly together, but still obscenely shredded. His face had been cut off in jagged streaks and slapped against the plant-encoded siding of my house. The plants held it up like little macabre hangers to flutter in the humid wind.

They wanted me to find it, and to recognize him.

I shot it down with my pistol, and put it with the rest of his body. I buried him in the yard outside his house, with pictures of his kids and wife. The digging was hard, and the hot air pressed my shoulders down. I couldn't even dig very far. I was too afraid of fuel or power lines. Eventually, the hole was wide enough to flatten out what was left of his body. I used pieces of broken pavement and round rocks from gardens to cover up the dirt.

I wanted to say a little prayer for him when it was all finished. Too bad I don't know any. Maybe I'll think of something tomorrow. I only remember the beginnings of prayers, and never the endings. Tomorrow, I'll search his house for a bible. I just can't do anything more today.

I just can't.

Day 73

The old world, it's still as powerful as ever in my memories. It's almost August, and the drum has ruled for the last seventy days. I think about it every day. Usually, it's the first thought pulling apart my sweaty eyes inside the shed. Ling, my family, the glide of normal cars on sunny pavement, or the sweet sounds of airplanes booming across the sky - it all feels so distant and gone. Only in my dreams do they still have shapes and lines, and everything else in-between. I've thought about taking enough Benadryl so I can sleep and soak up the lost world, but it just seems so cowardly.

Plus, there's no guarantee it won't be an elongated nightmare.

I hadn't slept for three days until last night. I feel guilty about sleeping, like I should be in a supreme mode of grieving for my dear friend. My feelings are complicated about the matter. I want to cry more, to sulk, to be sad and lay around, but instead I'm just angry. He couldn't listen to me. He couldn't value my opinion enough to not wander out into the darkness and the plant-painted masks of the old world.

Portraits, murals, collages of old memories and lives are now living phantoms powered by clouds of pollen and spores. In all fairness, I might've been lured out by them if I hadn't watched those survivors try to enter one of those moving cars. If I hadn't watched the Unnamed appear and peel those people apart like fleshy oranges, I might already be dead.

I can't blame Gerald for wanting things to be the way they were. I want the nightmare to end every time I wake up in the morning.

Speaking of illusions, last night there wasn't single streetlight lit or buzzing spectral car. Nothing moved in fact, not even the wind, it was the first still night in the entire drum it seemed like. I don't know why the Unnamed halted all their activity for the evening, but I can't only assume they did it to make me wonder and worry about their next move.

Were they expecting me to charge out at them with some sort of rage and high-powered machine gun? No matter the level of grief I'm feeling from everything, I'm still not suicidal. Don't get me wrong, I've thought about it before. I've thought about it plenty. I have plenty of guns to shoot myself with, and they all work relatively well and fast. I still have respect for life. Even the Unnamed can't take that away from me. I don't want to die like Gerald did, surrounded by monsters jabbing and swinging theirs claws.

The stillness of the night caused me to sleep like a sack of flour. I didn't even wake up until around noon. There was a sour and slightly brackish smell outside the shed when I woke up. Snowy started to whine outside the door. It smelled like something familiar, but with a hint of rancid rot to it. I opened the door slowly with the black muzzle of my M16 peeking out. There was nothing, just lines of thick grass and twisted vines with bashful blue flowers. The smell still lingered on the hot air, and I followed its invisible trail all the way until my house.

I vomited with what I saw.

They had pulled out his body from the grave I'd dug. They left it in a bloody heap just below my front door, the exact place he was left the night before. His face was reattached to the house where it'd been previously. The flesh, blood, and muscle were covered with scraps of dirt. It wasn't an illusion, but Gerald's real corpse from before. They were removing the body from its burial spot, and leaving it around my house to torture me.

What were these things? Why did they think this way?

I took the body back to the hole I'd originally dug. I won't have Gerald's resting place be desecrated over and over again. I know they won't stop. I don't threaten them. I know they won't stop. I burned the body with some gasoline from shed. I made the fire high and long, so the heat would melt everything away. I couldn't be around it while it burned. The smell made me vomit, stagger, and nearly faint. After the flames died down, I covered the ashes with more pictures, dirt, and rock. They won't bother with ashes like they did a body. Will they even be able to sense the ashes and fragments there among the dirt? I wonder why they did this. It was already enough that he was dead and that they'd killed him. Their tricks had worked. I won't be intimidated by their lack of respect.

Let us see what the monsters can do with ashes.

Day 74

No ashes on my doorstep this morning. Last night, the whole of the darkness was quiet and sulking, like I had ruined the fun for one long midnight. I didn't sit up against the crack in the shed like I normally do with the safety off my M16. I actually put a pair of headphones on as I slept.

My dreams were uneven, sweaty, and full of lost images from the pre-drum world. Last night, I dreamt I was staying in a hotel I traveled to when I was ten or eleven. My dad used to work in Honolulu at their mall when I was kid. He'd fly back and forth all the time, and stay in a brown-carpeted condo by himself with a Japanese VCR and old Star Trek movies. I'm guessing he watched "The Wrath of Khan" all the time.

He could never get into "Star Trek: The Next Generation." I always wanted him to, but when my father didn't want to do something he'd become an immovable force.

We'd stay in this really nice white-pillared hotel called the Moana Surfrider on Waikiki beach. The hotel was nearly eighty years old, but still a snow-painted jewel.

A disheveled, yet towering Banyan tree ruled its courtyard, and rained hundreds of large nut-fruit hybrids down on us.

We'd spend our days dodging downpours, counting stylish Europeans, eating pineapple, and sampling the snack-bar Teriyaki burgers. My dad would insist we watch the sunset every evening. He'd look so happy and dignified watching the fiery orb dip down into the leveled blue-cut horizon. His wily beard and

189

thinning air making him into a sort of sage, like someone who knew a lost secret about the universe.

I'd give anything to see him right now.

In the morning I didn't do anything but read some more "Calvin and Hobbes," and let Snowy roam around the jungle-bursting lawn. The grass has spiked up past my knees now, and beneath the bristling spears are tubular highways of hardened vines.

Snowy doesn't go very far, it's too hard for her to navigate the boiling grass. She likes to sit in the sun and pant. When Ling and I would take her outside on hot days, we'd laugh about how strangely comfortable she'd be panting in the heat.

At least someone is happy about the new environment.

Around two p.m. we wandered out into the neighborhood. I checked Gerald's grave for tampering, but there weren't any signs of the Unnamed. Maybe they could only sense the blood and not the ash. We walked around the neighborhood two or three times, circling the same blocks and billowing trees. I just didn't feel like going any further.

When I walked back towards the shed I thought I saw a little kid running away between a pair of houses. He was short, brown-haired, and covered in dirt. Snowy barked at him as he ran away. I wouldn't have minded talking to him. It wouldn't be strange or weird like my previous interactions. After hearing Gerald die, I don't care about being awkward in this new apocalypse.

There can't be very many of us left.

Day 75

Last night, the illusions were back and flowing through the hot darkness like some sort of phantom train. Their false sounds and fake melodies kept me up most of the night, so I decided to just watch them. I know they're out there waiting for me, to cut me to pieces and empty my skin, like some sort of floppy flesh-soft toffee. That's what it looks like when the Unnamed are done with us, flat and red buttery candy.

I shouldn't dwell on the gore of it all; the trees still bend, the wind still blows, and I'm still alive.

Who else is alive?

Watching the illusions last night, they were alive. They were moving and glowing in the darkness like fresh pieces of fruit. The warm kitchens, the bumbling cars, the distant twinkle of classical music. What makes them? What makes them so lifelike? I know it's the plants, but which ones? I'd burn them if the Unnamed didn't notice. They notice everything it seems like. I mean they're lapses to their scouting, but not many.

It would be easier to live without hope due to their perfection and viciousness, but they're not perfect and that gives me hope. It's almost a hidden weapon knowing they don't come out until the drum. The daylight breeds this type of wonder, and you buy into it hoping the nightmares will take a day off.

It'll never happen. I know that. Now I just watch the illusions through a metal crack in the shed like some dreaming toddler. I'll take the illusions and their pieces of the old world, like sparkling little pieces of eye-candy. I'll take the way life use to be, anyway I can get it.

I didn't sleep until early morning. My dreams were terrible, a bunch about Ling, Gerald, and my family. They were in dark clouds, like the spores from before surrounding the monsters. I've dreamed before about my family, plenty of times in fact, too numerous to count. I haven't had one single happy dream about the people I've lost, not one. Once the plants are gone, and the world has been bathed by fire, then I might dream normal again.

No it won't be possible, it's impossible. There is no wave of fire to take the jungles away. No magic bullet, no special weapon, there aren't any more troops even.

After my morning nap, Snowy and I walked to the lake for water. The fluke Unnamed I killed, the one that brought all the misery and basically killed Gerald, it's corpse has completely vanished into the carpets of twisted vines and trickled leafs. I couldn't even look at the playground we hid in. It hurts too much. I found some bullet casings on the ground. They shimmered under the humid sun like a couple of metal Mike and Ike's. I never should have made us hunt and kill it. The Unnamed was a glitch, a misguided spawn, it never should have existed in the daylight.

And I never should have killed it.

I swam in the lake. It was nice, clear, and cool. Snowy came in with me into the shallows. Her little body wiggled awkwardly in the sandy depths, and her black snout popped up just through the thin layer of bobbed water. She looked like a little sausage submarine.

We splashed and played, then sprawled out on the beach. The white rolls of sand kept most of the vines at bay, so it almost felt like a normal surface. You forget what it feels like to walk and sit on ground not swarmed by plants. I watched the clouds for a while, and I imagined fortresses, castles, and walls, anything to keep the Unnamed out. Their reflections look so timid and natural against the water. I miss reflections.

On our way back from the lake I saw the kid again, he's clearly following us. He ran between some houses on our way back. I caught sight of his eyes. They were blue and glowing like little lost gems of some begotten innocence. I remember seeing children when I first started raiding houses. Before, everything seemed so desperate.

Now everything, every empty house and distant piece of sunlight, looks broken and lonely, like us.

TIMOTHY

Day 76

They were back again last night, the illusions. The momentary pause given to me by Gerald's death has ended and the fake world has geared back into action. I don't care really, the illusions became even more inhuman the night Gerald was killed.

They won't be tricking me anytime soon. The show is staying the same anyways; orange lights in kitchen windows, buzzing streetlights, and the occasional car bouncing down the road despite the layered plants and their pavement dominion.

Any logical thought applied to the situation of the drum, the plants, and the Unnamed would make the illusions explained, and not some dire mystery painting the dark.

Logic doesn't work in the world of the drum. The old style of life, the old digital age, it's just a few layers of ivy away. The layers keeping the old memories away aren't thick enough, they're not strong enough, to have some reserved hope that the world will suddenly billow about and the plants will wash away. Maybe once the plants completely block out the metal and concrete, survivors like Gerald will come to grips with their situation.

Military. I keep going over this particular word in my mind. The plants, the monsters, and of course the drum, they all came so sudden and so deadly I can't believe for a second the military was able to get organized. Judging from my travels around the Twin Cities everywhere was hit and mangled by the Unnamed.

The operation, the counterattack where I lost my other friend, didn't even mobilize until nearly a month into the darkness.

A surprise attack like the drum completely destroyed any infrastructure or semblance of organization. It's a brilliant strategy, a very brilliant strategy.

Just based on the strength of the word "military," you think everything will be okay as long as they exist.

During the pollen-produced play last night, I closely listened to the drum. The beats are heavy, but shallow, like the sound isn't willing to fully expose itself to the world. Yet, the thunder still wants to be heard. The sound mimics the appearance of the Unnamed, who have physical features like claws and ribs, but also are blanketed by a moving cloud of spores. The Unnamed want to be seen, want to produce fear, but with a sense of mystique. They know the mystery about them drives their power.

Fear is an excellent motivator.

This morning I didn't want to leave the backyard. I just sat at the entrance to my shed with my M16 and "Something Under the Bed is Drooling," the latest book in my Calvin and Hobbes binge. I keep skipping through the parts of summertime, which occurs often in these books. I'm stuck in an endless summer, and I don't need little reminders like these watercolor woods.

This afternoon, I had some more productive thoughts. I'm contemplating setting a trap with a wire and grenade. I've been going over the idea in my head over and over, like tying a shoelace. If I hook something up to the grenade's pin and apply some tension with wire or string, I'm sure the Unnamed will trigger it. I need to put the traps far enough away from my house to prevent suspicion. I also need to make sure no survivors are staggering around. I can't diminish the human population at all, that'd be a serious emotional setback.

I'm waiting for the kid to appear. Nothing yet, and the evening will be here soon along with drum. I want to talk to him, get to know him, I don't care about the awkwardness of the world anymore. Maybe he'll only appear if my back is turned? Tomorrow, I'll go for a walk again to Rainbow Foods and see if he appears.

It'll give me something else to think about.

Day 77

Last night, the world flashed back to when the drum first started. The nights where I'd hide in my basement and listen to the sounds of whoever wanted to face the Unnamed, before the world figured out they had no chance. Those nights were horrible, listening to the world writhing against the monsters like a pinned snake.

Every night, listening to humanity fight against a faceless foe, picking at that naive scab -- no wonder I feel hopeless. No wonder we all feel hopeless.

I'm not sure what happened, or why there were people moving through the area in the drumming darkness, but around midnight the shadows were flashing with popping gunfire and small explosions. I followed the sounds of the bullets, and they bounced off of everything in hollow glances and pings. A few even hit the shed. I covered Snowy with my backpack and put her around my chest.

I was so worried that a bullet would pierce the shed and split one of us open.

All I could do was hug her, and crouch down over the dirt. I hugged up so tightly to her, she would lick my face through the backpack as the thunder of distant mortars and rockets threw the tree branches everywhere. They sounded hollow and rocky like skeletons were trying to swallow up the shed and pull it away. A few times I shifted to the other wall, and buried us beneath the boxes of

supplies and gallons of water. Anything to stop the path of a bullet,
anything.

I heard machines rolling through the streets, hundreds of
them. The pavement cracked and moaned against their heavy
treads. The grinding was so intense, I thought the earth was going
to fall apart and my house, shed, and everything would be
swallowed up into a fiery jagged mouth. It'd be nice to go out that
fast. It'd be nice to avoid the shadows and wild claws.

The drum still beat behind the metal-driven whirlwind of
gunpowder and crunching chambers. I could hear empty bullet
casings clanking against the pavement. That sound would be
impossible with the plants having webbed everything over in green
tarps of vines.

I stay still the entire night as the shooting waged. Seldom
did I hear a gun or cannon stop firing to reload. It was like they
were spending every inch of ammunition on this battle. I know the
Unnamed aren't overt and present when you fight them. I've been
lucky enough to fight them in close quarters. At a distance, they're
nearly impossible to see, especially in the dark. How could these
people fighting them possibly know where they were hiding?

Around four in the morning, they finally stopped their
fighting and the world returned to the drum and the silence between
each beat. There were no illusions, or Unnamed sulking around the
empty spots of crumbled houses or caved-in walls. I stayed up all
night watching for them, but there was nothing. Only the bugs
brewed about in aimless clouds.

In the morning, I scouted the area for traces of the battle. I looked for bits of fresh rubble, empty bullet casings glittering in the sun, and scraps of torn clothes with inky blood beneath their layers. There was nothing though, not a single crater in the ground or pulverized wall from any of the nearby houses. In previous battles, I'd find this debris so fresh, it'd be shedding dust in the sun like wayward dandruff.

There is nothing though, no sign of the previous night's battle.

I walked around the block three times with Snowy, looking for the smallest, most minuscule signs of the battle. Nothing moved. Only the trees and layers of thick grass shook coiled, and enlarged, against the hot air and buckling breeze. The plants always look like they're ready to bubble and burst, like possessed sores from some unnatural botanical plague.

I stopped searching in the late afternoon. It had been an illusion, every sound, every random bullet, and every boiled explosion. It was all part of some massive trick by the Unnamed and their unseen allies in the gloom. When I wandered back home with a scared and worried Snowy, I saw the kid from before. He had been following me the entire time, dodging behind the houses like I use to do when I played with Nerf guns when I was his age. I bet he regrets any imaginary nightmare he played war in now, the apocalypse was real, and the old world was the subject of a perverse nightly trick.

"Don't get tricked by the battle, they're illusions too," I yelled, as he ran away from me. I hope he listens. I don't know why he always runs.

I'm not going to hurt anybody.

Day 78

No false battles dotting the gloom with random bullets and shells. No mocking mortars powered by spores, and no gear twisting treads clanking across the pavement. Last night, there we no illusions at all, not even the warm portraits of the old world. Strangely, I wanted there to be some show, some sort of movie to play through the tangled plants and pollen. Nothing though, the Unnamed must have exhausted all their energy with the elaborate battle yesterday.

I wonder if it worked for anybody, as in, did anyone actually go out into the darkness to fight. I never would have wandered out, even if the illusion had been real. It was too violent and bullet swept. Do they actually think those types of misconceptions are appealing?

I slept through the night. I even left out my earplugs and snored through the drum. I sprawled out fully in my shed, and Snowy slept right next to my face like a curled hotdog. She kicked me a few times in her sleep, but I didn't mind, it was the quietest night we'd had in the last two weeks. I had no dreams either. Dreams or nightmares, either remind you of the past, and that's more painful than reality.

This morning, we walked to Rainbow foods and the lake again. I didn't feel like wandering out into the green world, but I was hoping the boy would follow us and I finally could speak to him. I'm not that scary looking? Am I? My dog certainly isn't intimidating, and I usually carry a weapon around with me, but it's not like I'm pointing it's nozzle at every moving shape in paranoid swipes. If my mind would catch up to my situation, then I might be like that, but there is still this wistful ignorance working between my eyes. Maybe this feeling joins hand-in-hand with survival.

Maybe your best defense for the apocalypse is ignorance, a necessary ambivalence for the horrors around you. Let us hope this phenomenon occurs naturally, and I'm not just a big idiot.

Crystal Lake was quiet, clean, and trembling beneath the arid wind. The water looks so clean and lucid with the plant influx. I remember my dad saying he wouldn't eat a fish out of this lake if a gun was poking against his temple. Now, I bet the fish are happy to have all these plants oxidize the water and suck up the algae.

The bugs are happy too, they swarm everything now. I might as well be a moving buffet with the mosquitos at night. It seems like the drum, the Unnamed, and all the plants prodding their way into every surface are only interested in making us human's miserable, and nothing else. This targeting can't be some blunder, it has to be specific to the monsters and whatever controls them.

This has to be intentional.

I swam around with Snowy in the water for about an hour. I wasn't worried about someone sneaking up on us and stealing my supplies. There are plenty of guns sitting around. I've stored tons of canned food in the ground beneath the shed. If someone broke into the shed, they wouldn't even realize the shed was occupied. I store everything beneath the thin bricks of the floor. Even my blanket's go down there. I can't take any chances with anyone. One sign of wealth in supplies might attract marauders. It's in our nature to pillage, and there is no law anymore.

I explored Rainbow, but didn't find anything useful in the plant-caked aisles. I found some messages written on the floor in paint or blood. One was a daughter to a father and another from a son to his parents. Others were from parents to children. I couldn't read them very long, because I didn't want to waste my flashlight, or become violently depressed. On my way out of the shattered sliding doors and checkout lanes, I found one more message: "Dad, help me, I need you." The message had been spray-painted on with neon pink paint. It was from a child named Timothy. Something about it made my stomach feel light and worried.

On our walk home to the shed, I watched the roads and their overgrown edges. The grass has sprouted long and wild. The trees are heavy with extra foliage, and hang over the streets like an overburdened tunnel. The air beneath their endless eaves feels cool, but has an aura of viciousness to it, like the shadows could be hiding something. The ivy and tendrils wrapping the houses have become prickled with bold colored flowers with paper-thin petals. I know the flowers serve some purpose for the Unnamed, I just don't know how or what.

I didn't see the kid anywhere on my walk back. Not a single thing moved between the houses and trees. Only the wind stirred, like it has been since the beginning.

Day 79

Last night, the world was only partially alive to the strange images summoned by the drum. There were no streetlights buzzing phantom light in the gloom. No confused insects wandering about like lost kittens. No warm kitchens, bustling cars, or shadows of walking figures going from one empty room to another. There were no pictures to it all, but the sounds still echoed across the dark buildings in lost voices and harmonies. It was almost like the mirage-mixing-beacon that sputters up during the drum was out of sync. Listening to the voices chiming about the shadows without any light to give them shape was actually more terrifying than watching the old world glowing about.

I kept trying to find the images to match the sounds, but only empty alleys and dark houses looked back at me. After a while I gave up, put my headphones on, and went to sleep with Snowy next to me. I kept my gun next to my left arm with the safety off. Not that it would matter if the Unnamed suddenly realized I was hiding in this shed. They'd tear it apart in seconds. I wouldn't even stand a chance. It's starting to weigh on me, the delicacy of my hiding spot. I'll need to move soon. I'll wear out my luck here eventually, and it'll be game over for me.

In the morning, I started scouting around the houses looking for a new place to hide. I didn't find anything. I'd say 40 percent of the homes in the neighborhood have imploded upon themselves in green crumbles. The weight of the plants will eventually tear down everything we've built. There is no stopping them. Every day, the vines get thicker and more severe in their width. Every day, more ivy shuffles along the streetlights and broken down cars. Every day, the grass gets longer, harsher, and pickled with small flowers, which are so delicate, an oven-heavy gusts of wind can sever them like rotted cloth.

I couldn't find anything I was satisfied with. It felt weird and invasive to be living in a stranger's home, even if they were either dead or gone. I went in a bunch of basements, bloody bedrooms, and shattered kitchens. Nothing felt right. Trees had fallen on houses just like mine. The weight of their intense eves has toppled them over with their roots mushrooming up in brambly clouds. Occasionally, you can hear them fall over the quiet neighborhood.

At night, they never fall, I don't know why.

I'm sure the only reason I survived that first month was because the maple tree in the back of my house plowed through my roof and made it look derelict. The Unnamed probably didn't believe someone could have survived the house collapsing. The whole world is like a junk filled sink, which is slowly being drained out by the plants. It'll all be one level green plain. Imagine what the world will look like after one year, or two?

The dead wouldn't even recognize it.

I walked all the way to where the neighborhood ends and Highway 81 begins. The very last house on the left looked somewhat undamaged and in relatively good shape. It was a tall rambler, with an extra garage on its side. Barely any plants have coiled over it, and a few of the windows weren't even broken. The moment I started walking up to the house, Snowy started to whine incessantly in the wind. She wouldn't even walk up to the driveway, and her body started to shake so much, her tag jiggled.

"Hey! What are you doing here?"

It was the kid from before. He looked clean, blue-eyed, and was dressed in brown shorts and a blue t-shirt. They were strangely clean. He walked out of the front door like an offended schoolyard bully.

"Take it easy, I'm not going to hurt you, I was just looking around your neighborhood," I said.

"Why? Don't you get the idea? This is my house and you should just stay away from me."

The kid was a bit of an asshole.

"Well, I can, but are you okay? Are you hurt? Do you have enough food?"

"I'm fine. I'm perfect. Now leave me alone."

I looked around at the world and gritted my teeth.

"Perfect?" I said.

"Yes, perfect. Now stay away from. You don't want to know me."

"Well, there aren't a lot of us left, so we should stick together," I said.

"You don't want to know me," the kid screamed at the top of his lungs. The sound startled me and I almost pulled my M16 up just by reflex.

"You don't want to know me," the kid said again, and walked back into his house.

I walked back home shortly after the little conversation. Why wouldn't the kid talk to me? What had happened to him? Surely, even a child can see that the living must stick together. I racked my brain about it all afternoon and early evening. Right before the drum started, a few F14's flew overhead. I wonder what they were doing.

I wonder how many more times I'd see a plane rumble across the sky?

Day 80

Last night, the sounds came whistling through the darkness, but not the dreamy images. Something must be wrong with their mechanisms and motivations, like the Unnamed were being lazy or passive. Those are two adjectives I would never think to associate with the Unnamed, but these last two nights have been so pathetic, I can't think of any other way to describe them. More sounds, more bells, wheels, and piano songs.

No images to match this haunted orchestra. I'm not sure if I'm simply mad that the Unnamed aren't pulling out their "A" game, or thoroughly paranoid about the sounds just being there when the images aren't. Whatever the case, I'm so angry I can't really think about anything else in terms of the night. I actually stayed awake worrying about the next step, the next round of nightmares.

I hate feeling this way.

In the morning, I ate some canned goods. Mostly cans of tuna, but I also had a can of string beans. I ate a little bit more than usual, hoping it would help my state-of-mind. I gave Snowy a few extra treats too. I know mentally she's probably okay, but if I get to indulge, so should she. We're in this together, and if weren't for her, I would've killed myself a long time ago. Is it weird to think about it? To visual how you would do it? What weapon to use? How you would hold the trigger? Things have been so dark and confusing, sometimes confronting the very end gives you relief, and it makes you feel what a bad idea ending it might be.

When you pull yourself out of this pit, this hidden abyss wandering about the inner sanctums of your soul, you feel guilty for even thinking about it, and it's that guilt which keeps those thoughts at bay. I've started to think about this alternative less and less.

I'm going to set traps.

I'll put them up about an hour before the drum starts, further north in the neighborhood where I haven't noticed anyone or anything living or moving for weeks. I'm afraid a survivor, dog, or even cat might hit my trap and kill itself. I'm not sure how I would come back from such a scenario morally, but it'd be awful. I'll need to scout out the area a little bit more closely in the effort to avoid such a tragedy. I'll set just one, a wire with a grenade attached to it. I'll put it between some thick plants, a spot where humans or animals wouldn't normally walk. There aren't many stretches of pavement or grass where it isn't hard for us to walk anymore. I'll have to be careful, so very careful about where I put this trap.

The problem with the kid from yesterday was also vexing. Why didn't he want to talk to me, or get to know me? There are so few of us now, we must stick together. Forget about all the perpetual worry from our dead and postponed culture, and worry about surviving the drum. I guess Gerald couldn't even come to that conclusion himself so why should a child? I shouldn't have written his name down in this notebook. I'd been avoiding it. It makes me too sad to see it, just too goddamn sad.

In the afternoon, I walked back down to the house. Snowy came with me, and I kept the safety clicked off on my M16. I'm trying to think of a time I haven't had it clicked on? The kid was sitting outside his house on the stoop. He was playing with a dried hunk of vine. It looked like a strip of dried skin, with green sparkling flecks of dandruff. I've never seen anyone play with a hunk of the plants. It's a weird sight. It's very unnatural looking. I never would've thought to play with the plants in any form. Snowy immediately started to snarl the moment we walked towards the house. Something is up with her recently.

"What do you want," the kid said, breaking the thick roar of the wind.

"What's your deal kid? Look around there isn't many of us left, stop being so grumpy," I said, with some surprised angst.

"Doesn't matter, don't get to know me, it's a waste of your time," the kid said.

"I don't care. I've barely known anyone the last thirty days. What's your name kid?"

"You're not going to find out. There's no point in trying to find out."

"Yeah, there is, we're alive, and the world still turns. So tell me your goddamn name."

"I have a gun. I'll shoot you and your dog. Just walk away from me."

I pull my gun up abruptly and step in front of Snowy. No wonder she doesn't want to go near this little monster.

"What's your deal? I'm just trying to help you."

"Me too, now get away from me. If you shoot me, nothing will happen. Not a thing."

"I'm pretty sure something will happen, and I will shoot you if you threaten us again. Stop acting so crazy."

"I'm not crazy."

"Then why are you acting this way."

"You don't want to know. You're a survivor."

Something gets caught in my throat.

"What? What do you mean? So are you?" I stumbled.

"No, they know about you. Now walk away. I don't want to know about you at all."

"Who, who knows about me?" Something in my lower intestines comes loose, like I want to soil myself.

"You know who, you named them." The kid won't look up at me as he plays.

"What did I name?"

The kid throws down the shredded vine and stands up at me.

"Go away!" he screams. It's loud enough to rival the wind.

Snowy barks at him. The air has a strange mixture of haste and chaos to it. In less than a second the boys inside his house and mixed away into the darkness.

"I'm going to be setting some traps on the north side of the neighborhood. Don't go over there if you can help it," I yelled at the open space.

The boy approached the door and shook his little head.

"It doesn't matter," he said with a pair of faraway eyes.

Day 81

Last night, I'm not sure what happened, but the whole darkness was swimming with the Unnamed. I could see their spiked forms drifting through the shadows. They were neither concretely visible, nor completely invisible, but like sinister silhouettes from some distant and effective nightmare. They haven't billowed about the black spaces between my houses since Gerald was killed, and I slaughtered their random strangler in the daylight. I did slaughter it. I like that verb. It makes me feel more potent than I really am.

If anyone is aware of their shortcomings, it's me.

Every twirled plant, every booming beast-thunder in the night, and every humid breeze reminds me feverishly that I am a meat sack, a walking feast for vines and bugs. It's a dark method of thinking, but sometimes wallowing in the hopelessness makes you feel accomplished, and honest. Sometimes admitting your problems is the only way to like them. I'm helpless to the drum and the Unnamed, pure and simple. I've been lucky in my encounters with them, but I'm still just a child with a toy gun and a panting dachshund.

They were all around me last night. I hate it when they do that. They shook the walls of the shed with their footless dashes. The roof of my broken-down home creaked maddeningly against their perches. At times, I could hear their claws clink against surfaces as they ran by, like horror-hollow wind chimes. I swear they know where I am, and just like to tease me like a wolf with a lame deer.

In the morning, the plants around my shed looked high and green, like the latest tramples of the Unnamed had given them a fresh vote of confidence. The air was still steamy, heavy, and so sweetly pollen-heavy, it felt like you were locked in your grandmother's cupboard, but without the nostalgia. Some days the sweetness is worse than others, but it's most certainly not natural, in fact it's gamey like sour rotten meat. Sometimes you get that acidic sweetness on your tongue, and you can't get rid of it no matter what you drink or eat.

Today was one of those days.

I wandered to the northern parts of the neighborhood today, where the bigger houses are holding up a little bit better to the writhing layers of plants. I'd love to torch them all. It'd be a nice and long fire. The houses are big, and sound with all aspects of the old world vanities in the neighborhood as it crawls into Golden Valley. I crawled up a tree with Snowy in my lap and watched the long trail of fading concrete between rows of these lumber giants. Nobody moved, no animals roamed, the whole area was completely and utterly empty. Only the shuttering shadows of the trees haunted the daylight like paper-cut phantoms.

It's weird. I almost wanted to see someone hiding in the houses. Not only so I wouldn't feel alone, but it would give me a reason not to set my traps. I'll come watch the area tomorrow. If nothing moves, I'll set two traps in the vine-sewn lawns of a couple half-crumbled houses. Everything seems to be at least slightly crumbled these days. In fact, the only house that isn't crumbled is the one the antisocial little boy is living in.

That goddamn kid.

It's so strange to me that he won't talk to me. I'm very perplexed by it. There are so few of us, doesn't he understand the nature of our situation? If I could only explain it to him as coherently as I can to these diaries. If I only could make him see everything we've been through, and how our species can only survive through cooperation.

I walked down there today, but I didn't get too close to his pristine house. I saw him sitting in the exact same spot, with the same exact plant-husk as yesterday. I stood about a block away and yelled, "I'm setting traps tomorrow in the northern part of the neighborhood, don't walk around there." He turned to me and shook his head.

"It doesn't matter," he yelled back. I knew he'd say something like that.

I waved at him with a relaxed swing. I'm not going to let the little bugger irritate me anymore than I already am. To my surprise, the little kid waved back with a sincere white smile. He quickly retreated into his house, like he'd just broken a local neighbor's window with a baseball.

That was something at least. Something normal in our interactions.

There are clouds on the horizon as the evening grows. Hopefully, it rains and drives the Unnamed into hiding, and their illusions can't form. Plus, we need the rain. It was something my dad would always say. It makes me feel good to say it. We need the rain.

Day 82

Again with the Unnamed. They were everywhere last night, every little and big surface shook and rattled to their glides and dashes. It drove me silently crazy in my shed, to the point that I wanted to fire my gun randomly into the dark like a crazy blind-man.

I kept control though, I didn't want to, but I did. I don't know what's making them bristle so much, making them want to take over the night even more than they already have. I can't idly sit by here, and wait for my mind to grow thin like overspread jelly, and come apart with a burst of yellow gunfire into the darkness. I'd be pulverized, mashed, slashed, wrecked, and mutilated within moments.

I've seen it happen, and it's not pleasant in any shape or form.

Nights like tonight, where they run rampant like unabated clustered-monster storms, they are the most difficult. At first, I couldn't ignore the illusions weaving among the darkness like old television shows on public access television. Now, knowing their falsehood and spore-ridden interior, I don't even gasp at their spectral glows. Now I can dismiss the illusions as desperate tricks, as a strategy that must take place because the Unnamed lack the proper skills to hunt us when we're hiding. I don't mean to insult the dead who have been magnetized by these images, like my dear friend Gerald, but please tell me you see the plants and monsters around you?

The Unnamed have dominion now, and it will be this way for many nights, because the plants grow thicker and sharper with every sunrise.

Today, I went to the northern neighborhood with Snowy, and watched the still houses with my safety off and my pistol next to my foot. I don't know what caliber it is, but it must be good because it's heavy, and accurate. I'm sitting on a broken down car that has been dyed a bright green by the plants. It was a van, but the tires have been popped, and it's sinking into the pavement. Its high enough up for it to be a good vantage point, and an overgrown tree sits behind me giving me shade. Snowy sits next to me like a little log, sniffing the air occasionally with a dignified snout. What does she smell? Surely, in this new environment, the spores have a scent too. She must smell them with a typical regularity, which is why the illusions have never really interested her.

I watched those broken down houses for a good four hours. Nothing moved except the trees, and their swaying popcorn-shadows. It was good enough for me, the block looked utterly deserted. I jumped down from the van and picked two spots to place my traps. The first was in front of giant two-story home with cracked bay windows. The other spot was across the street in front of a half-burnt out rambler.

I wonder how the fire was put out

I brought along my biggest and sharpest kitchen knife to cut a hole through the vine-tight underbelly on each lawn. It took about ten minutes, and my hands got raw and stingy, but I eventually managed to carve a two foot gap in the layered plants. I wrapped a wire along the pin of the grenade, and a sturdy vine connected to the grass. I covered up the opening with the scraps from my cutting, and repeated the process across the street. I left Snowy on top of van, much to her whining dismay. It would be too dangerous to have around these grenades and wires.

I had them all placed and ready to go by six p.m. I didn't want to stay out there any longer than that, even though the drum usually doesn't start for another two hours. I grabbed Snowy and ran back to my house. I saw the kid running too, as I turned around. I wish he would stop acting so strange, and talk to me.

There are so few of us now, so few.

Back at the shed, I got everything ready for the night. I'm contemplating digging my hole deeper so I can hide inside of it better. I started working on it the other day, and it'd be a good long-term plan. The clouds from last night, they haven't moved all day. They look like a grey wall frozen against a sharp blue plain of ice. It's really weird, and there is plenty of wind. I don't know very much about weather, but I know this is very, very, unnatural.

I don't like it.

Day 83

Last night, they were around me again, like a spiked-storm caught in some magnetic spin. I couldn't believe it. It's never been like this without cause. I could understand the anger with me killing the grunt. The weird Unnamed caught in the sore and sour daylight, and how that might provoke an unwholesome reaction. I keep going over that day in my mind, each painful and frightening detail, how the monster didn't even realize we were there, until I shot its body with the rifle. Then everything clicked, and the Unnamed jumped into its purest form, a killer and masher.

I'm sure they'd love to pulverize me, and mush me down into a sinewy pile of faceless guts. I bet they dream about it during the day, like I dream about them being wiped off the face of the earth, like a lovely weed whacker had been swept across the planet's surface. I find it hard to believe they wouldn't dream about killing me. It'd be nice if I was that important to them, but I'm probably just a flaky piece of flesh in their grand wheel of sand.

I listened to them stalk and hunt all night. The wind howled too, plus the drum thundered away in the distance like a lifeless marching band. Someday, I'll find out what that sound is, what warped instrument summons the Unnamed. When I do find it, I'll burn it to the ground, and take the ash and wipe it along the pavement in huge smiley faces.

I want to take everything blooming with this plant-rumpus world, and melt it down into ridiculous shapes. I want to remove every aspect of the Unnamed's monstrous appearance.

Plain and humble dirt would be nice, if we could just grind up all this plant matter and sprinkle it along like dust.

These fascinations of mine help me get through these long nights, especially when they sulk in the shadows waiting for too loud a breath or cough.

In the morning, I was still pumped from the adrenaline of last night. Having them around keeps you awake and alert. I used that extra energy to dig deeper below my shed. I judged the ground around the shed, and where the old power lines and gas lines might run into the ground. I carved out a five foot deep square. The hole was just big enough for me to kneel down inside with Snowy. I'd keep the opening hid with some mats and carpets from my house. All my food, ammo, and water have been hidden underneath the ground in various damp cubes. You never really know how paranoid you can be, until you're thrust into a post-apocalyptic setting.

After I finished digging, I walked down the block towards my traps and the northern part of the neighborhood. The clouds were still frozen about fifty miles away like napping giants. The storm looks stuck and suspended by some celestial force. They were probably just afraid of the Unnamed, and didn't want to bother making their way over these glowing green fields. I know the natural world has been turned upside down, and new laws are taking effect around us.

I found my traps loose and unused in a small pile outside the van I'd been perched on yesterday. They were in perfect condition, and the wires had been delicately unwrapped and unhinged. It almost looked like when you'd find old computer wires at the bottom of a box after cleaning your garage or something. They were covered with a yellow and grimy dust, like they'd been dipped in some honey-like pollen.

I cleaned them off and brought them back to the holes I'd made, but they were completely sealed and healed from the day before. The plants are beyond resilient, but I've got nothing to lose by trying again. I placed the traps just above the first layer of plants this time around. I don't want to keep cutting apart these coiled layers of flower and weed. Maybe I'll have a better chance of hitting one on the surface of all these strained and shackled vines.

On my walk back to my shed, I saw the kid again. He was running away from me. It's so frustrating. I just want to scream at the little brat. He stopped as he ran away and counted the houses with his fingers.

"Hey kid?" I yelled, slightly dashing after him.

"What, what the hell do you want?" He said, squinting his little eyes in the sun. The plants hummed against the wind around us, and I heard something chattering in the distance.

"If you ever need me for anything, you know where I live. I'm in the shed."

The boy suddenly collapsed to the green-wrapped road, pounding it with his fists in shaky blows.

"No, no, don't tell me!" He screamed against the humid, pollen-full rolls.

Snowy started barking and I lowered my gun at him.

"Don't go there, I won't be there," he screamed to himself.

He smashed his fists between the vines and petals wildly.

"Listen, I--" I tried to say, but the kid just snarled up at me like a feral dog with plants hanging off his teeth.

He then started to back away from me shaking his hands.

"Don't say anything to me. I thought I told you that?" Snowy started to roar. This was new behavior.

"Stay away from me," the kid screamed again, and charged down the street. He was like a fading glimmer of living light in a long and lost green tunnel.

Day 84

They came for me last night.

The drum started hollowly and assuredly, and the amber twilight bled down along the blue sky like a vanishing jet's foamy tail. A dimness took over the stars, and a strange air filled the shed. Snowy started to whine wildly, and crawled against the tin flap of the shed. She started to scrape at the walls frantically, clanking her black-white nails and smacking her body underneath the space between the wild grass and metal edge.

I wanted to scream at her, but I couldn't make a sound. Any loud human sound would attract them like a cloud of rabid terrors. I scooped her up and pressed her to my chest to keep her calm. Her body shivered so wildly I could feel it numbing my rib cage through the leaden Kevlar. There were no sounds around me. The crickets were quiet their string-stretched song. The wind was weary, unable to brush a single knee-high blade of grass. I was too scared to move. The air around me had eyes to it, like even a heavy breath would be seen through these flimsy walls.

Then I heard them.

If they hadn't rushed all at once, there would've been no way of knowing they were coming. The ground shook to them, their phantom horde, and the walls clanked to their sharp clouds. Without even thinking of an escape plan, strategy, or even basic logic, I dropped into the hole I had just dug, and quickly covered up the top of it with the pair of awkward carpets I'd found. Snowy howled as I jumped in clumsily, like an overburdened bird. I

accidentally smashed her face against the opening as I jumped in.
She yelped horribly in the soil-soft darkness.

Then they came through the walls.

They smashed through them like toy strips of plastic, like all
forms of gravity and force were at their complete beckoning. The
ferocity of the pulverization caused the hole to crumble in on us like
stale and powdery bread. I couldn't move forward, backward,
downward, or upward. The weight of the monsters overhead sunk
the earth down on us. Snowy started to cough and sneeze. I held my
breath as the dirt clamped and spread along my sweaty face. It
glued itself to me like a high-powered mold.

I heard them twisting things, the roof and walls of the shed,
and anything else they could sink their claws into. Metal cracked
and shattered like empty stale bones. Boxes were shredded, supplies
crushed and squirted. Anything above the dirt was completely
eviscerated and pulverized, like they couldn't stand one atom of my
existence. Sickeningly enough they were silent, deliberate, a force of
unspeakable focus and concentration. I soiled myself inside that
hole, I could feel the warm urine run down to my toe.

I thought I was going to die there.

Then, the carving stopped, like a boney switch had been
flicked off inside their devilish gears. The weight shifted above my
head, and several distinct hisses filled the air, and then vanished in
nightmarish echoes. They'd left. They were expecting my body to be
there hiding safely amongst my paper walls. They knew, they had
intelligence, and I know who gave it to them.

He was right. I should've stayed away.

I stayed in my tomb for twenty minutes, coughing dirt and choking dust. I held every sound I could in, and kept Snowy so tightly pressed against me, our frantic heartbeats synced up. I knew we couldn't stay there for very long. We'd suffocate beneath the debris and dirt like unfinished corpses. I listened for them between the thuds of the drum, and nothing stirred in the dark.

I couldn't stay there.

First, I sloshed my head back and forth as I stood upwards, making a small path for me to see through. I pushed the dirt away with my lips and tongue, until my head broke through a little split of crushed metal soil.

The night was still there, along with the star-buttoned sky. The air, though humid and thick, felt cool against my face. Snowy squirmed the moment I broke through. I rolled my shoulders through and set her next to me. Her muzzle was all bloody, and she was shaking.

I was so angry.

I couldn't do anything.

There was an Unnamed, one of the big ones, right next to me. It was obviously a sentry, a watcher to see if I had survived the attempted mutilation. It was at least eight feet tall, with a long cloaked back of flowing dark spores. I could see its long and mutilated claw, the kind that grows in an instant and can tear apart tanks, dangling into the dirt just five feet away from my head.

Glances of gold light shinned off its skeleton, and the hood with its faceless mind mixed in the suffocating darkness.

Oddly, it didn't see me. I wasted no time, and pulled myself free in the most silent and clumsy way. I had set Snowy down, but she immediately froze and stuck her paw on my boot. She couldn't move. I quickly scooped her up and placed her in my backpack like a half-cracked egg. I crawled away from the blind giant and into the alley with the half-smashed houses and their sunken roofs. Every shadow made me squirm and swing my M16 around.

There was nothing though, they must have other victims to hunt.

I eventually made my way down the block. A few Unnamed drifted by as I crawled, moving in sharp swings of inky light. I wanted to fire at them and end it all, but I couldn't. I can't just give in. I crawled into an abandoned garage with a shattered van, and twisted motorcycle. A tool cabinet had been flipped over and covered with the leafy ivy. I squirmed underneath it and watched the grassy alleyway.

Nothing moved, or even tried to. The house behind the garage had imploded from the plants, but a part of the roof still remained and had fallen down like a broken tent. I smiled, and started to crawl towards it. Four Unnamed, the smaller ones, flooded into the garage. I stopped my crawl and watched them float past like snout-less wolves. I plucked a grenade from my belt and pulled the pin out with my teeth. It was a hard gesture while being on my stomach. I threw the grenade awkwardly behind me into the

228

alleyway. It rolled, bounced, and went silent next to a smashed house. The four demons spun around and glided over the tool cabinet. The black air behind me suddenly rocketed apart in a steamy combustion. Hisses filled the air, and without even thinking I stood up and looked at them.

They were just in front of the explosion, the fire from the grenade had caught the plants. They were flailing about, trying to put it out with their invisible hands and slab-sharp claws. They hated fire, I knew it. I threw four grenades behind them in consecutive subtle swings. It's all I had. They clanked behind them as they fought the fire. I quickly crawled underneath the collapsed roof, and watched the four little harbingers sizzle open like volcanic bursts.

It killed all four of them in a popping instant, and threw the fire all over the plants. I sunk deeper beneath the roof, into the furthest shadows I could find. Hisses and shapes filled the night. I was too deep under the roof to try and watch them take the fire away.

I was just glad they had to worry about something.

I stayed up all night watching the darkness beneath the roof. Nothing wandered into the sight of my M16. I was ready to fight them. Ready to die beneath a stranger's broken roof. Nothing came, only a few heavy and stagnant bursts of humid wind.

In the morning, the moment the drum stopped, I walked to his house. Snowy was walking again, and I had cleaned her mouth with some water from my canteen. She had a slight limp, just like me, but was okay considering the circumstances last night.

His house was clean, quiet, and free of the impending waves of plants. I walked up to it with my safety off and my finger on the trigger. The kid was sitting on the cement with plain skin, still eyes, and folded hands.

He wasn't surprised to see me.

"What are you?" I said, getting ready to pull the trigger.

"What?" he said without looking up.

"What are you? I'm not screwing around kid. I almost died last night thanks to you."

"I didn't do anything," he said leaning back into the deep darkness of his open front door.

"Yeah? Is that so? How come a literal horde of the Unnamed came rushing into my shed the day after I told you about it and you went goddamn nuts?"

"I told you not to tell me anything, not my fault."

"If you told me what was going on, I might've been a little bit more cautious."

"What's going on? You think I know?" The kid laughed.

"How come they knew where I was from telling you, it doesn't make a single bit of sense."

More hot wind raged, which was trailed by broken teal-horned petals, billowing across the clean cut home like a witches spell was powering up. The trees bristled angrily, like I shouldn't even be there talking to this monster. I wanted to shoot the kid, but *this was precious moment for me. He was clearly linked to the Unnamed, that much was certain. I relaxed the M16 in my arms and flexed my forearms. He noticed my change in posture and smiled at me waving the husk of plant.*

"You can put the gun down, you can't hurt me, I'm not even alive," he said with another little laugh.

"What, how are you not alive? Are you one of the things that comes out at night, with the music, the lights, all those fake pictures," I said.

"Yes, yes one of the those, I'm a poser."

"How are you that? Why would you be that?"

Snowy snarled at him behind me. She knew all along something was very abnormal with this kid.

"I'm going to kill your dog," the kid said methodically raising his pistol.

I fired my M16 with myriad of clanking bursts. The little person in front of me shattered into a broken cloud of yellow spores and sticky pollen. It almost looked like a cloud of dried honey had exploded. The spread of sunshine smoke reincorporated together in a familiar hissing sound. The same song they made last night when the grenades burst against them. In just a few seconds, the kid was again sitting on his stoop with a gun pointed at me. He was an illusion, a broken down creation of the Unnamed.

"Still need more proof, human?" the kid said putting his weightless gun down on the concrete.

I couldn't say anything at that exact moment. It was another terror, nightmare, another beast from a horror.

"I don't understand, I just don't understand," I said.

The boy spun the strand of plant around in his fingers and shook his head some more.

"Nor I human, it wasn't supposed to be like this," he said.

"You're a monster then? Why haven't you killed me?"

"I'm not, just a watcher, a scout, another set of eyes for them. I'm not even supposed to be here. I was supposed to come out at night. That's when they killed the boy, the one they made me after."

"What boy? The one that lived here before?"

"Yeah, he was Timothy or something. Timothy tried to kill himself and failed. He couldn't move very well. It was only a matter of time."

The boy got up and looked around. I stepped back some, trying not to soil myself again. It was like a puppet-string had twisted his personality aside, so he no longer had to be in one character."

"You like his house? It looks like his doesn't it? Before we polluted it as you might say."

"Another illusion? How are you doing this?"

"I don't know, I said I'm just a glitch. A random and uninvolved voice in the daylight. They know everything I see, but I don't tell them anything."

"They? Who's they? The Unnamed control you?"

"Yes, your name, I think it'll catch on."

"How? Where are they? What's happening?"

The overstuffed maple tree above me, rustled together like a deep breathing storm. This whole conversation was unnatural, and the natural world was letting me know with all these violent twitches.

"I can't tell, and I don't know. I'm sealed away and sewn shut. Now they use me whenever they want like an old baseball cap."

"You must know something then? Who are the Unnamed? Why are you doing this?"

The kid sunk his head down again.

"They have me too tight, I can barely speak."

"How do they have you tightly? I don't get it?"

The kid shook his head with frustration, swaying like an unsound wall.

"I'm so between things you see, when I was made they took some of his gestures, and now it's all mixing up," he said.

"So then what are you? I'm getting really tired of this goddamn shit. I need to know what they, you, and everything is at the very goddamn least."

I wanted to shoot the ghost again, especially since it didn't even bother him, except for possibly hurting his pretend feelings.

"I only know confusing things, and I'll tell them to you because I feel sorry for you. This boy knew you, watched you in the neighborhood, and you could've helped. He doesn't know why you

didn't. Now he's dead and I'm an eye, an appendage, something to report back to your Unnamed. They come to my house when the heartbeat begins, and I tell the shadows everything. Then I vanish and appear here in the morning. I was supposed to lure you out at night, but the system glitches and I am in the sun. The Builders never wanted this to happen."

I wanted to scream, but I only stood still, trying to keep the skin from melting off my body with panic.

"Builders? What do you mean builders?" The very nature of the word made me squirm.

"I can't say anything more, or I'll be pulled back into the shadows. The boy wants me to stay alive. I'm not fond of being a toy and ghost." The kid twitched his head like a cracked doll. He stood up suddenly and backpedaled into the dark, eye-socket of a door. There are no objects inside the house with any discernible light or shape. The darkness pooled behind him as he walked in, like he needed to heed its wormy and wet reach.

"Hide well tonight human, but don't tell me where. Don't you dare do that," his voice trailed off into the hidden abyss.

There was hissing at the end of it.

I ran back to my shed to salvage what I could, and to find a new hiding place.

Day 85

Last night was long and arduous to say the least. After my first chat with the little monster-illusion-boy, I ran home to salvage the shed and any supplies. The plants had coiled over it in glowing-green bunches and threads. They don't waste any time on repopulating their areas. The shed looked so strange flattened to the ground, like a literal giant had walked out and smashed it with its plant-bright foot.

We're just lint to them, scraps of meat with no real purpose.

I salvaged a bunch of food and water from beneath the shed, but first I had to hack away at the plants, which was like chopping wood without an axe. I used my best kitchen knives. I was exhausted too; all the shadows of the previous night had worn me out. The conversation with that thing, Timothy, was exhausting too. I kept playing the word "builder" over and over again inside my brain. Building requires intelligence, and the builders were separate from the Unnamed, they had something controlling them. What would control monsters? Something human, something like us who would create something to kill and conquer. I might be thinking too much, but I can literally think about nothing else.

I took all my boxes of food, water, and ammunition back inside my house. I crawled through the broken stairs from weeks ago, and down into the hollow wall I knew so well. The wall was torn open, and plants had grown inside with vapid hands. They knew I was there, and came looking for me one night. The basement looked so desolate with the white morning light, which was kissed

and dusted with scraps of pollen. For the first time since this whole
ordeal, I felt homeless. I took my supplies back upstairs and stored
them in a closet. I don't think they'd bother with this hallway door.
It was too out in the open to arouse suspicion. They probably have a
knack for scouring out hiding places now, so an obvious spot will
probably go undetected.

At least that's what I'm telling myself.

Snowy and I spent the night underneath the same roof as last
night when we were nearly slaughtered. I decided to keep it simple,
and not look for another hiding place right away. The visibility
beneath the roof wasn't ideal, and I was on my belly the entire
night, since the structure is too low to the ground. I couldn't see
much more than the alley's grass pavement and the bottom of a
telephone pole. The drum started up like normal, and the thunder
felt a little louder beneath the roof and its canvas of vibrations. I
fell asleep from pure exhaustion and nothing else. I was still
terrified. The conversation haunted the tail end of every thought and
worry.

How was this possible? This detached ghost a block away
from my house, reporting every night to this unseen enemy.

In the morning, I stopped by my house and checked on my
supplies. They were still there, stacked up in boxes and bins in my
old closet, like the apocalypse had never even happened. It makes
me sad to look so normal, so impervious to the plants, drums, and
demons. It made me vomit. I don't know why.

I had dreams about the Builders, though I couldn't really identify them or see them. There were just voices in the houses, echoes of people from my past, my father, mother, and Ling. It made me all so sick. What could they possibly be? They had to be separate from the Unnamed. Timothy, who is their phantasmal mouthpiece, he named them specifically, like he had to address them at some point.

What could they possibly be?

I walked down to his house again after I ate some food, fed Snowy, and attempted to wash everything up. His house looked so clean and inviting from a distance, an irregular chunk of non-plant rotted material. Someone else will probably see the house and be tricked by the human-devil. I need to set up some warning, some sort of sign for people to read coming through. Tomorrow, I'll scout out some spray paint and leave a message on the pavement or something. People have to know he can't be trusted, even though I want to talk to him again. I miss talking. I miss it so much.

I'll hide below the roof one more night. Tomorrow I'll find my new spot and then approach Timothy again. If I phrase questions differently, maybe he'll answer them without tipping off the Unnamed. The clouds have moved a little bit, but the storms are still frozen, like a waiting dishwater-grey maelstrom. We need it to come. We need it to wash away the spores and all their little eyes. One last thing before I crawl beneath the roof and the drum starts. What darkness is behind that little monster? The house must be connected to their world, their shadows and hidden doors. I know

237

there is something there worth investigating, but how would I even get close to it with him there?

I know the darkness behind his front door was hissing, just like them, just like the Unnamed.

Day 86

Another night inside the broken down roof. Again, I couldn't see a single thing beyond the shattered shingles and leafy tatters of the house's broken roof. Everything has become so crumbly, unkempt, and debris-happy since the plants started to collapse everything. You can hardly walk a flat step on the pavement without a nest of crumbled mortar, or stalking plants tripping or stabbing you.

I watched every shadow that sneaked by in footless little bounds. They were still looking for me. I must be a ravenous target of theirs. I've evaded them thus far, mostly by luck, so I imagine my reputation must be literally blossoming among the Unnamed community. Notoriety would be much better than popularity in this situation, since every day I'm fighting for my life and fluids.

They won't bring out the illusions until they've truly given up on me for the time being. I need to find a new hiding spot instead of this flat space beneath this bread-chunk of roof and tar. It'll be too risky once the illusions start up again. They'll be too many sounds, manipulations, and spore-happy paintings illuminating the tight shadows. Snowy had been good about stifling her enthusiasm for the old world, but I'm still afraid she might bark at one of those phantom cars as they swing by in bright turns of classical music.

I ate early in the morning, and fed Snowy right away. I wanted to preserve as much of the day as possible to find a new hiding spot. I narrowed down the possible candidates fairly quickly. It couldn't be any houses, since each house probably had some sort of marker for the Unnamed to notice if it was now being occupied. It couldn't be some place with open walls like the roof, since the illusions might instigate my loyal canine friend. The shed had worked because it was out in the open, an obvious spot in the midst of the green world. I had to find something similar to that, something unassuming and non-threatening.

It also had to be in a spot where that ghoul of a little boy couldn't see me.

I walked across the neighborhood most of the day looking for a spot. A few homes collapsed in wooden claps and sprinkling metal as I walked. I'll never get use to their buckling groans. The whole neighborhood looks like someone took can of bright green silly string and sprayed it down over and over again. Coils, strands, ropes, chains, flowers, petals, pollen-pockets, and everything else in-between covered the roads, houses, lamp posts, and cars.

I didn't find anything to my liking.

Eventually, by early afternoon, I was back at my house and staring at the remnants of my old shed. Staring at the metal wings of my old living space, a reflection from across the alley caught my eye. My dead neighbor's van, the one do-gooder who boarded up his entire house by the third or fourth night, was still partially intact. It was a big, navy-blue conversion van he hardly ever drove. The roof to his yellow garage had tilted over from the plants, sending the van onto its side in a shattered whack. Plants had partially overgrown the side of the van, but the broken windshield which faced the smashed garage was free of any vines. The van looked dilapidated and unusable. A few trash cans sprawled across the front of the van like fallen statues. I cleared the cans and glass away from the windshield and explored the inside. It was completely clear of any debris, and the windows facing skyward had been blotted up by the plants so no one could see in. I put a small tarp in front by the windshield to make the inside of the van dark and unused. From the inside of the shattered windshield, I could set the cans up like unused little sentries.

It was my new home.

I moved some of my supplies over, but not very many, just stuff to get me through the night. The inside of the van was warm and dusty, and I spent a few hours clearing more glass out. The interior was navy blue with pillowed cushions. It was full of old Harley magazines. I stacked the magazines up against the windows. I'll take every defense I can get. After I finished, I made sure that little devil-kid wasn't watching me. I doubt he will, since he was internally bothered by his traitorous ways.

I will talk to him again. I just need to formulate riddles so he can talk without vanishing. This is a precious moment to get to know him. I must take advantage of it.

The darkness, I'll figure out what it is, I'll know its weakness.

It's almost evening now, and I'll be hiding in my van soon enough. I can't stop playing that old SNL sketch in my head with Chris Farley when he would say: "in a van, down by the river." I actually laughed at this a little bit in the orange-evening gloom. I don't remember the last time I laughed. It'll be a rough night here. I'll figure out if this was a good spot pretty fast based upon the Unnamed's reactions.

Tomorrow, I'm going to speak to that little kid again, and maybe learn some more about the Unnamed. Also, I'm going to set more traps. They'll be all over the place. I have to unsettle them. I have to keep them all away. I hate them. I hate them beyond anything. I'm no fool. I won't vanish like all their pretty toys. I have worth. I can't let them walk away unhurt, and hunting us down like walking blood-clots.

I have got to do something.

Day 87

It was weird last night being in a different place. It's like when you sleep on your bed and your head faces a different direction, or when you build a fort as a kid and sleep behind the blanket walls. Granted, my situation's quite a bit more sinister than switching your sleeping arrangements. I wish my life still had this lost subtlety to it, those lovely mindless movements. Now, every day and every object gets related to survival, to buying more time before the thundering drum rolls together in passive echoes in the twilight.

The drum just hasn't stopped. Every night it's there, a siren's song of crackling percussion, a heartbeat to some lost green-laced monster.

It must be some plant-wild hammer. A drum layered and pumped by these ferocious botanical forces.

Last night, the Unnamed didn't find or bother me in my new hiding place. Inside, the van felt dusty, blue, and sticky with this sweet upholstery aroma, which gave me a headache. My neighbor must've barely used it. The van was turned on its side, which meant all the passenger chairs were sticking apart sideways in a bizarre fun-house posture. The plants blotted up the outside windows pretty good, but the moonlight still managed to sneak through their blemishes, dropping narrow rays of clean blue, like little errant flashlights. It made the inside of the van ghostly, and persuaded with supernatural forces. It made it feel with time and dust, like nobody had touched it in years.

It'll take a while to get comfortable inside of it.

The Unnamed moved around the van a few times throughout the night. Their shadows would bloom up through windows in murky, fast-paced outlines. It was almost like their shadows were having a hard time keeping up with their movements. They were still hunting me. They were so close the other night. The frustration must be tedious, even for faceless monsters. A few times I heard their claws scrap against the metal of the van as they wandered by. It sounded like an old echo in some empty house, a labored ache between some seldom used floorboards. Everything about the Unnamed is haunting. I'd actually prefer their illusions to them stalking about in their wispy, bladed forms.

I barely slept at all in my new spot.

In the morning, I fed us right away, and then walked to the western side of the neighborhood, close to North Memorial where Gerald and I had explored. I didn't see a single thing the entire way, no animals, no recent tracks of weary boots in the thick and overwhelming grass. Nothing, not a single thing.

How many of us are left?

I set some more grenade traps inside the thick grass bunches just outside some houses. It looked like nobody had been here for decades. I set four of them. Two in front of a white house with a caved-in wall, like a soft skull had been cracked. Another trap was in front a blue house on a little hill. The place still had windows, but strangely no roof? It looked like a disheveled old man had just woken up, and the broken white siding was his wild, smoky hair.

I made sure that little demon brat wasn't around when I placed my traps. He must've disabled them during my first attempt. He's their complex spy, an unwilling demon in their nightmare parade. He must have remnants of his original personality left inside that illusion. His former body, and whatever the Unnamed did to him must be linked through a conscious strand. It all sounds like bullshit, but the science of what's going on doesn't really matter anymore.

Only survival and hiding from the drum is important.

I walked to his house after I was done with my little trap setting. I thought I heard a planes dull roar billow across the sharp blue sky. I scoured it looking for the silver angel, but I couldn't find anything in the noon sun. I wanted to find something. The storm to the north still looks frozen in time, like a painting with a dead painter. We need the rain, and my water supply is growing steadily smaller. I'll have to set up containers to capture it. Easier said than done.

The demon-boys house was clean, clear, and old-world looking. If I had thought about it all before I met him, I would've realized how wrong its appearance was in this green world. I was just so happy to see another human being after Gerald died. I would still be happy to see another human. I'm not even sure what I would do.

The air around Timothy's house was warped dirty and sticky with humidity. Walking up next to it was almost impossible, like the moisture was a sticky shield of pollen-dusted matter. I couldn't even

*get close to without breathing heavy, and Snowy wouldn't even
approach it. She just sulked down on the ground with her crooked
tail between her legs. Something's happening with this house, like
an otherworldly hole has been attached to it.*

*Of course, the little monster-boy wasn't there. He was
probably out hiding or stalking someone. I really need to make a
warning for other people passing through not to trust him.
Tomorrow, I'll go scavenge around Rainbow for some spray paint.
I'll mark some of the big buildings at the onset of the neighborhood.
He has the potential to kill everyone who comes through here, even
though, from what I gathered, he doesn't really want to.*

He's a nonliving contradiction.

*I watched the moving darkness inside Timothy's brown
doorway. He left the door open, and the void shuttered and twinkled
behind the clean siding. It was hypnotic, like a string of ocean
waves constantly piling over themselves. At times, it almost felt like
the darkness was going to come bursting out of the door like a
harshly contained breath. Snowy kept on whining behind me as I
watched the shadow-door. Something inside of me felt light and
airy, and without hesitation, I threw a grenade into the eye-socket of
a doorway. I ran away with Snowy underneath my right arm and my
gun pointed everywhere. I ducked behind a crushed car and waited
for the pop of static, the chemical explosion.*

Nothing happened, not a goddamn thing.

Day 88

They popped, fizzled, and boomed last night. I was so happy, so happy to hear my traps scar the night in orange bursts. I pictured them twinkling like little captured suns in the drumming darkness. Booming away the harsh spores and nightmares circling the plant shadows and all their sharp forms.

To be more specific, my grenades went off last night.

It happened shortly after the drum started, and the twilight sunk into the coiled plants, which smoked with a brambly perspiration from the days' worth of sun. I listened between each vine-taunt thump of the drum. At first there was nothing, just the irrational buzzing of crickets, and thwacking of moths against the cracked sides of the vans. Then my traps clapped and exploded in the darkness, like distant sulfur lullabies. All four went off in a matter of minutes. The Unnamed must've been heavy in that area, like they'd been watching me and knew where I was walking earlier in the day. Paranoid thoughts like this wouldn't even be possible or relevant, if I hadn't met Timothy. I wish these fearful ideas would stay rooted in theory.

Nothing can be discounted, everything could be a threat, and paranoia might be the only thing keeping me away from the golden tips of their built-in claws. Who built them to be so savage and cutting? Timothy mentioned Builders. I wonder what they could be. Are they like the Unnamed, or are they something else? Only questions for now. Only questions inside my dusty van with sharp shapes moving around the moonlight.

It felt good to get back at them.

Besides my traps finally being triggered, nothing else really happened last night. I expected the Unnamed to rub up against the van again, and the scrapes to drive me silently mad in my blue upholstery prison. Nothing though, not a goddamn thing. You would think the Unnamed might be at least temporarily interested in me after the traps, and flood my backyard and alley with their broken shapes.

There was nothing, no retaliation.

In the morning, we checked out where my traps had gone off close to the hospital. There were a few pieces of shrapnel sitting around the mushroom holes inside the lush plant-skin. It hadn't repaired itself yet. I wonder why? Snowy and I then staggered down to the lake for an early morning bath. It felt good, and the plants around the lake had stemmed their green tide. The water was clear, inviting, and lacking any real traces of the Unnamed and their environment. It was almost like a little trip to beach. The sky was clear too, except for the frozen storm, which looked a little closer today, like a boil ready to pop. How are these plants surviving with so little water?

I stopped by Rainbow on my way home, and sifted through the cluttered darkness of dried up diapers, cleaning products, and smashed shelves. I found some neon orange spray paint to write some messages with. I also found some more dog treats and canned vegetables. It's hard to believe this place hasn't been pillaged into an echoing empty space. I almost wish it was empty. That way, I'd at least know other people were still alive and roaming around.

I sprayed the sign at the edge of the parking, which was a narrow brown column with vines crawling up its brick sides. I sprayed: "Don't trust the little boy, stay away from him." It was hard. The spray paint felt like an angry snake locked into a tin can; therefore, my message looked like a seven-year-old trying to write a note to his teacher. I'll make a few more tomorrow. I feel better for doing it.

On my way back to my house and the van, I walked by Timothy's house. He was sitting outside, and playing with the same scrap of ugly weed from before. Snowy instantly started growling and wandered behind me. I was carrying my rifle for once, or Gerald's rifle I should say, and aimed it lazily at the little boy on the step. He smiled at me like a little crow, and shook his head at me.

"Come to stare at me human?" he said without really looking up. The darkness cooled and buckled in his doorway. How is it connected to anything?

"I've got more questions for you," I said.

"I can't answer any questions, but I can have answers to compare to answers."

"So what does that mean?"

"It means human, I won't answer anything unless you come up with answers yourself."

"Why won't you answer anything?"

"I'll be taken away. They're patient with me in the daylight already. I can't rock the boat."

"Rock the boat? The Builders will get rid of you?"

The boy shook his head some more. I hate it when he does that.

"I can't answer, this boy still wanted to live."

"He's dead, how can you know that, or anything?"

"He's not gone in all parts. We've sewn him into me."

"I don't understand."

Hot wind hit us suddenly, it nearly knocked me off my feet, and the trees shuddered layers of cotton-willow seeds.

"It's fine human. Come back when you have answers."

I aimed my gun at him again and debated pulling the trigger, just to watch him disappear and vanish, like when you rewind a VHS tape.

"Go ahead human, grenades don't work either, the darkness just laughed at you."

I really wanted to pull the trigger.

"What darkness?" I said trying to keep calm.

The boy smiled and pointed the dark portal behind him. It was the first little boy gesture I've witnessed out of him. If darkness could glow with pride, it most certainly was in this strange household.

"It likes you," the boy said with an ear to ear smile.

Day 89

After the creepy conversation with the little paramour and his weird attachment to the Unnamed, I hurried home and prepared for the drum. I'd cut it close by going to Rainbow and spraying that crude warning on the marquee. I didn't like running away from this weird little boy, but something about that sly grin made me so uneasy, I just had to run away.

Last night, the Unnamed didn't move at all, just like the night before. The drum sounded in the deep. It shook and stretched the shadows beneath the evening light, like little trickles of water caught between some sharp stone. They're waiting for me to make a mistake, to slip up when talking to Timothy, or make a false move in the night.

I'll never move unless I have to, unless they come storming through the glossy windows of this overturned van. I'm worried about the lack of escape routes inside this vehicle. If I had to, I'd shoot a window out and crawl through it, but they'd catch me before I'd get outside. This dilapidated van is a tomb. It's only a temporary hiding spot in these muggy nights. I'll need to find a long term solution to this situation. Having an extra place to hide within my hiding place saved my life. I need that loophole again.

The morning was scorching. The plants keep capturing layers of dripping condensation, which steams slightly against the curled curtains of hanging vines and twinkling ivy. It'd be a pretty sight if this miasma wasn't attached to monsters, phantoms, and illusions. Occasionally, when I stare at the unchecked greenery, I lose all the negative connotations about this world, and admire the power of nature. In just three months, the whole of civilization has been bracketed by these unwholesome plants, like all our cement and mortar were structured dreams.

I can't get past this thought, it keeps repeating in my mind. Everything keeps repeating. You'd think hiding from monsters wouldn't have a sense of boredom and routine, but it does, every day it does.

I pulled some grenades out of my hallway closet and walked back to the western part of the neighborhood to rig some traps for the coming night. I varied where I put them; in front of a rambler, a park, a parking lot, and random pockets behind the parking ramp of North Memorial. I rigged every trap in the thickest of leafy brambles between cracked buildings and overgrown grass. Nothing would wander here but the Unnamed, nothing else would have the strength to walk through such thick jungle floor.

I set nine traps to be exact. I'll have to start scouting for more grenades. I'll have to go back to the scene of the counterattack, where all those stupid men and women fought like caged meat for wolves. There are probably still plenty of weapons sitting around. There aren't enough of us to carry them.

After I set my grenades and traps, an interesting thing happened in the sky. First, there was a crackling sound, like fireworks were being launched in the narrowest of thunders. An inky layer of clouds spread across the blue from all corners of the atmosphere. It was like some invisible wall had been broken down,

and all the clouds rushed in like a thick fleet of smoke. The air
instantly became dark and heavy, like night had just collapsed on us
from the heavens. Something about the swimming darkness made
me cringe. I grabbed Snowy and threw her into my pack. She
whimpered and shook inside.

I could feel it through my Kevlar.

Something wasn't right. Whenever she freaks out and
shivers, it usually means the Unnamed are involved. I immediately
ran towards my house's block, and my overturned sanctuary of a
van. Rain started to fall suddenly in enormous sheet-clear claps.
The first strike of the water wall knocked me off my feet. The rain
was so hard, and so wild, it felt like I was in a swimming pool with
a few suspended air pockets. Running was difficult, and I didn't
want to slip, then fall on my back and crush her. I reached the
intersection for the road to my house, Drew Ave North, and stared
down the road at Timothy's cursed home.

Despite the rain, wind, and trapped drops on my long
eyelashes, I could see what was watching me from the edge of his
house.

The Unnamed, a smaller one, standing like a spiked stream
of captured fog. It looked dark, moving, like every fiber on its body
was alive and unwilling to stay still. Its hood stayed shadowed in
the rain, even falling swats of water kept its face hidden from view.
It crouched down as it looked at me, and those golden blades
popped out of its spore-dark hands like obedient little children

It was alone, sent to kill just me, and ready to attack.

At first, it did nothing, like it didn't want to move a single inch in the rain. It looked sinister, but slightly obscene, like something was off about it appearing without the drum's velvet echoes. The sky was completely dark, the wind was weighed down with the rain, and I didn't dare move as it stared me.

A hunter, sent from the household abyss behind that little boy's door. It might even be the little boy for all I know. He's connected to all of it, an extension of their leafy dominion and eviscerating shadows.

I leveled my gun at the Unnamed. Thunder broke the air, and the sky came apart above us in layers of spiked lightning. The gun felt so heavy, like I was carrying steel firewood. Snowy thrashed wildly inside my backpack. I crouched down with the point of my barrel aimed at the monster.

It still didn't move, and I wanted it to. Then I could fire my M16, until the clip went empty, and this clawed shadow would collapse into a mysterious spore cloud. I didn't have my shotgun with me, just my handgun. I don't even know what type it is. I know nothing of guns.

I've thought about walking to the library.

I kept my eyes on it. The rain acted fused with the air, like I was staring into an aquarium, like time was frozen by it, and even the layered drops of water stayed away from the demon.

The awkward butt of my gun was tangled in my backpack as Snowy scrambled up. I squirmed slightly and looked down wiping water off my face. Snowy whined immensely and stepped on my foot in the blinding water.

"Run, get the hell out of here!" I said.

I looked up with the round tip of my gun and the Unnamed had vanished into the storm. I needed to hide. It could follow though, stalk me to my hiding place and kill me in the real darkness of night. It could be a scout of sorts, some type of thing to find where I hide during the drum. It might not have the gumption to take me down by itself.

We quickly ran back towards my house. I watched every space that melted by, every quick gush of soaked plant and broken down rubble. Nothing moved. I wanted it to attack. I wanted to get it over with; especially, if I died. I didn't want that moment to last long. I didn't want Snowy to see it happen. I just want her to be okay.

Then I saw it running towards me. It was sprinting from between two collapsed houses, with water pouring off their debris-ridden roofs like cluttered fibrous gutters. Everything has become cracked clutter and old-home fragments. I stood my ground, and fired the M16 at it. It sprinkled and shattered about the rain in disjointed fluxes. The Unnamed shuttered underneath the bullet-powered string like seized black fog. Its claws swung wildly up to block the attack, and a few bullets fluttered into the rain like wounded silver birds.

It takes a lot of shots to kill these things. A weird combination of luck and invulnerability.

255

Before I even knew it, the Unnamed was on top of me. Its first slash with its right golden claw crashed through my gun, causing a burst of black sparked fire. It knocked me off my feet and scorched my chin and left cheek. It ran and jumped on top of me swinging downwards, but the rain made it slip, and I rolled away. I had my handgun out and fired it into the writhing cloud on the ground on my left. Snowy barked at it in tortured howls. She knew she was helpless against it, but she hated it nonetheless.

I fired the whole clip at it until it snapped empty.

It stopped and looked me in the rain. I saw a mask behind its dark and dotting cloak, which captured the clear color drops deluging around us. It had eyes, black, carved eyes like a lost statue deep in a museum. Something about them, something about their roundness made me shutter. They looked human almost, a face mostly sharpened by unseen strands, but the dark outline of the mask was there, and they were certainly eyes.

It tackled me in a weakened jump, swinging its claws like gold chunks of flattened ice. I fell down with it, and pulled my six-inch knife from my belt. I stabbed in its golden chest, clanking my blade against it until something snapped and cut my hand. It couldn't carve me. It couldn't carve me. The air was wet. Its body was heavy. I don't think there is anything else I can remember.

I woke up hours later to Snowy licking the blood and burnt skin off my face. The Unnamed was gone, taken away by the layers of grass, ivy, and flowered stars. It didn't take me? I don't know why. The rain had stopped. Everything was pooled around me in silver circles and edged droplets. My gun was shattered, my knife had split, and the blades of the Unnamed had dug up the pavement behind me as it tried to kill. The gouges of shredded rock were almost a foot deep.

Snowy whined for me to pet here, and I obliged as I coughed from the wounds on my face.

It was at that moment, that exact moment in the orange, fire-thin sunlight of dusk that the drum started deep in the coming dark.

I ran to my van with blood-weary legs. The shadows were ready to snap loose, and hunt me.

Day 90

I thought I'd be dead when I made it home last night. The drum was sounding in its fullness when Snowy and I ran down the street. The shadows all around us were twirling like inky strands of dark ribbon. They were unhinged, and untamed. The wiry world behind the shadows, and the Unnamed were about to come spiraling out of their hiding places in sharp and blood-happy geysers.

The thousands of reflections from the silver pools of the afternoon downpour glimmered in tight vibrations against the drum as we sprinted. Could they see me from the water? Did they know every panicked footstep I was taking? The puddles could hold them like the mirrors did before, and they'd see my hiding place and come tear me to bits in front of Snowy's spinning eyes.

I can't dwell on the monstrosities. They've swallowed enough things of my old life wholly and completely.

I just needed to keep running, and not look back at whatever might be stalking me. The rain, as if it were waiting for me to wake, started falling in irregular drips and drops. Pretty soon the entire rubble jungle around me was pattering and tapping, and thunder rolled overhead from the contained storms.

I wanted to scream and lay down to wait for one of them to cut me apart, but I didn't.

I kept running through the rain, until I saw my house, and rounded the corner where my front door had been torn off its hinges. I jumped over the crumpled metal pile where my old shed once stood. I rolled on the ground and crawled across the vine-wormed earth to my tipped over van. I inched between the smashed vehicle and garage wall. Water was pouring now. It fell onto my face, stinging me where the gun popped apart earlier from my bout with the Unnamed. I stopped a second and looked around before crawling.

Nothing moved. No Unnamed and no illusions. I wanted them to, I wanted them to still be there, and that way I would know, I beat them.

Nothing, the evening light was a blue-grey beneath the storming layer of clouds. Water streamed and gurgled down in hearty smacks onto the ground from all the broken roofs, buildings, and trees. Air felt cool, clouded, like it didn't know what to do with the paired hydrogen and oxygen coursing down through it.

It was almost like the earth had forgotten what it's like when it rains.

I crawled into the van, which was mostly dry except for a few leaking spots up by the windshield. I cleaned my face off with the rainwater, and tried to bandage it best I could. It was hard to see in the fading light, but I think I got enough gauze on to stop any immediate infection. The skin was flaky, red, and sore. It peeled whenever I turned my head too fast.

Nothing moved but the rain. It sounded clean, invigorating, and lovely. I didn't want it to end; therefore, I didn't want to sleep and wake up to the same dry plants pouting against the morning light. It's getting harder and harder to remember those few days before the drum started where nothing happened, and reality was still absent the Unnamed. If I think hard enough, I can remember them, but it takes longer, and the details aren't as vibrant as they were before.

I stayed up all night listening to the rain and thinking. The Unnamed sent a solider after me, a killer in the daylight to carve me up. I killed it in the most desperate way possible. I thought they'd be out hunting me in the rain, but nothing moved, not a goddamn thing. The rain probably messes with their cloaks of spores, making them much more apparent in the darkness. They don't want to hunt if they can't hide what they really look like. This vanity was keeping me alive tonight. No wonder they hate the rain, and throw up invisible barriers in the lower atmosphere.

The rain stopped around eight a.m. Fog smoked up from the plant-heavy world, and the smell of pollen was choking and stagnant in the early sunlight. I slept when the morning hit. My dreams were empty, dark, and occasionally interrupted by a violent breeze pushing down between the trees. I'd open my eyes and look down at Snowy while adjusting my stiff jaw. She'd just stretch out, and stick her little arms in the air.

I woke up around four p.m. I spent the afternoon looking around my van for signs of the Unnamed, but nothing seemed unusual. The plants and their thousands of vines, flowers, and pollen-clusters, looked extra coiled and sharp. I wonder if the greenland world was offended that it's grunt didn't take me down the night before.

260

I moved supplies into the van, and cleaned the blotted wound across my face. It stung beneath the alcohol. I wanted to scream, but I wouldn't let them have it. The Builders, whatever they were, had sent one of their children out to me, and I killed it with my bare hands. I kept repeating this statement in my head. It made me smile and feel warm on my shoulders.

I walked down to the spot of our brawl from the day before. The plants had a lump to them where we fought in the road. It was almost like how a snake looks when it's gorged itself on the lumpiest of prey. I was fully armed, with a spare M16, and my shotgun strapped to my back. The safety was off my gun as I walked. If the Unnamed from yesterday had been a little bit more patient, it would've had me.

For fun, and morbid fear, I walked down to Timothy's house to see if he was outside, or if he could maybe explain what the hell happened in his weird riddle language. I stopped half a block away from his house.

It was gone, the clean and sterile abode. Plants wrapped and warped with leafy tendrils and sprinkled ivy. Flowers twinkled in colored gems along its smashed roof and broken windows. The entire thing had been reclaimed and adjusted back to this green hell. I stared at if for a good hour waiting for something to move.

For some reason, whatever reason, I started to cry.

Day 91

Last night, I didn't sleep. This world, our old world, has become so warped and diseased with this invasion of plants and monsters, I can't stop thinking about it. My mind doesn't even need to make nightmares. They're all here, blooming around me every morning, and drinking my blood like dew. Some days, its complete boredom, not a single thing happens in one way or another. Then, in one night of the drum, I'm scrabbling for cover from unknown monsters, and praying beneath moonlight in an old van.

I don't know why I miss him.

He was a monster after all, an extension of those things, and a slave to the Builders. It's such a simple goddamn name for something so inexplicably horrible and bloody. I know Timothy was a monster, but to call something so villainous and terrible "Builders." I don't get it. Inside their collective, their hive, or whatever grim colony operates the Unnamed, something told him to call them Builders. What could it have been?

Days and nights, nothing happens, even with the drum sounding in the deep. Then, the shadows swarm, people die, and reality seems caught in this fluid vacuum of phantoms and illusions. Every day I wake up, thinking the dreams are part of this reality. It always takes a drop of sweat below my eyelid to sting me back to the present time and place.

At least I haven't dreamed of my family recently. Sure, it's nice having my sub-conscious paint their pictures for me, but then I wake up and want to vomit.

It hurts so badly all the time, having these people come and go, even if they're monsters.

The Unnamed were quiet last night. The drum boomed and broke through the darkness. Bugs banged and trotted along the grey-blue shell of the van. Snowy slept curled at my feet as I sat against the vinyl-cloth hybrid of a seat. I still keep the safety clicked off my gun at night. Snowy can sense them coming, but the whole Timothy vanishing thing has really got me on edge.

I stayed up all night. When the drum stopped, I wanted to curl up and close my eyes, but I couldn't do it. I immediately jumped up, woke up Snowy, and walked down the street to Timothy's house. I actually ran there, to see if the world had changed back to its pre-drum gleam.

I was immediately disappointed. His house was there, but not the clean-shaven version with a haunted portal. The green version was back, and the siding looked more dilapidated than yesterday. I walked up to it and stared in the broken down front door. The darkness was gone. No black cloud sat contained between the walls. I could see the entryway. It was coiled with vines and dotted with red flowers. A horrible stench was trailing out of the doorway. It smelled sour, and salty, like something was decomposing at an alarming rate.

I wanted to go inside, but Snowy started whining the moment I walked up to the door. Then I started to shake and tremble. For some reason the wind was quiet when I approached it.

Why do I feel like the wind is always watching me?

What was the deal with this house? What had it been attached to? I ended up running away from it after a few minutes of staring into its overgrown doorway.

Maybe tomorrow. I need to know. I need to.

I walked down to the lake. I needed to get away from everything, and the lake was the perfect location to do so. Snowy and I took a little swim, washing away the sweat from the previous days. We played in the water, and I got her to follow me out to the deeper end of the shore. She paddles so funny with her tiny legs, and her little nose sticks straight up just past the water, allowing her to breathe like a tiny submarine.

We played there all afternoon. It was a nice way to forget everything.

On our walk back we passed Rainbow. The crushed cars in the parking lot, from the first night, have been completely encapsulated in plants, like awkward green pills. The entire parking lot is littered with flowers, trails of vines, and sheets of trembling ivy. It's a literal sea of green.

I want to burn it all to ash. Every last piece of it.

As we walked back I noticed the marque from before where I spray-painted the warning about Timothy. Another message was scribbled below it in sky-blue paint, it said "Thank you!" Someone had come through and heeded my advice. I looked around to see if anyone was watching me, but the whole world looked empty and glowing, a weird and eerie contradiction.

At least someone else was alive.

On my way back, I walked by Timothy's house again. I shivered as I walked by, and got goose-bumps along my forearms. The moment I stepped passed it, I felt like someone was following me, or right on my heels. It made me run back to my hiding spot, whatever it was. Something was there, I could hear something breathing.

It was the most hideous sound.

Day 92

It all came back to life last night. The illusions, pollen-thick and wild, glowed in the darkness like unchained images from our plant-imprisoned world. Streetlights, houses, and cars speeding by with music trailing out of their down windows. Lights even turned on in my house, and two dark figures walked back and forth in the kitchen, opening the refrigerator and cabinets nonchalantly.

With what happened with Timothy and all the monstrous anomalies so far, the images seem even more false. I know my kitchen is covered in vines and flowers. I know the windows are smashed from the fallen tree and the roof has been caved in. I know I can't even walk through my house in a straight-line, because the floors embedded with lengths and lengths of vines.

How foolish do they think I am?

The dark portraits didn't start until a few hours into the drum. I've been considering keeping track of what time everything starts, but I feel like it's all so random, it'd be a complete waste of energy and time. The drum and images are most certainly related, but that faraway thunder doesn't determine when the fake nightmares spring up. I wish it did. I wish all things were a little bit more predictable. Instead, it seems like day after day with echoing drum feeds this abnormality, and the world keeps getting darker, besides the glowing unchecked growth.

I slept for the second half of the music and show. It was nice. Snowy curled up next to me and snored soundly. The drum and images don't bother her anymore. She's actually calmer about the whole situation than I am. Why are they hunting just humans? They know nothing else is a threat? How could they possibly know that?

They are the living incarnation of violence.

It was around two in the morning when I heard the sound. At first, I thought it was an unusually massive moth smashing against one of the van's windows out of confusion with all this incorrect illumination. The sound continued in meaty slaps, like someone was trying to get my attention. The darkness was being watched, I couldn't just answer the proverbial door, and let whatever it was inside. The Unnamed would come, and I would be pulverized into a muscly red pulp.

"Use your voice, say something?" I said to the van's side. I whispered it just enough to drift through the thin metal. The pounding stopped. There was a long scratching sound, followed by a heavy drag. Whatever was outside the van couldn't walk, or move very quickly. If it was a human, it would've been spotted already, and torn to pieces.

"I can't open the door for you, they'll come inside. Hide till morning, and meet me here when the drum starts," I whispered in the darkness.

More dragging. I could hear something rubbing against the pavement repeatedly with the same force and direction. Something was being marked outside the van. Snowy was awake at this point, and started to whine beneath a few blankets. Dust and heat glowed inside the van with hints of moonlight. Time came to a complete stop as I watched the shadows.

There was a mumbling sound, like someone was trying to speak, but couldn't even attempt to make the basic motor function. The dragging started again, and became quieter as the drum filled in the shadows. I listened as close as I could, but the sound was gone, it had vanished into the gloom.

I didn't sleep the rest of the night.

In the morning, I expected to find someone to be outside my van wanting to talk to me, but there was just sunlight, steam, and dribbling dew. I inspected the spot where the thumping had occurred on the van. There was a bloody hand print dried to the van's blue side. Small trails of condensation had disheveled it, but the hand print was small, like that of a child. Below the mark was this crude, hand-sized "T" scribbled onto an open spot of pavement. It was written in gritty and faint streaks.

I knew exactly who it was for.

Snowy and I walked down the block carefully. I kept the safety off my M16, and watched the empty spaces between the jungle-heavy houses. Nothing moved, just the humid air broiling about. I reached Timothy's house. It was still corrupted with plants, and no longer the mirage hub from before. I approached the broken down doorway, and stepped carefully over the coiled plants.

Nothing moved, not a goddamn thing. The smell hit me again, that sultry, yet, sour aroma attached to rotting food and meat. It pushed me backwards when I first entered the house. There was blood trailing to the living room. I could see the fading dried marks along the plants. Snowy wouldn't come inside the house with me, so I tied her to the door with her extended leash. She walked to the very end of it, and sat on the street.

I turned a flashlight on and walked into the house. The whole thing was covered in vines and flowers. You could barely see the scraps of wallpaper behind each living column of plants. I shuddered at them as I walked. They were almost pulsing in the thick heat.

That's when I found him.

It was Timothy, barely. It was just his torso mostly, with no legs attached. His body was ripped apart in red gashes, but they had been sewn back together with strips of bright green vine. He had scraps of clothing still, but they were blood-rotted and dark. His left arm had been cut off, and had a tourniquet of more vine. His right arm was full of greens stitches, along with his chest. His eyes were sewn shut with flowers, along with his mouth.

A few shiny tears twinkled out of the blood-dry eyes. His right arm was trembling with pain and confusion.

"Timothy?" I said.

His body shook wildly as he tried to sit up, but he couldn't maneuver his torn apart body. He mumbled something from behind that sewn face, but I couldn't understand it. He shook with more tears.

I couldn't see him like this. It was beyond anything I'd known from this point on.

I pulled the trigger without a second thought. If I had thought one moment more, I wouldn't have done it. I would've tried to save him, which would have been wrong.

I fired seven shots into his head and body. I wanted to make sure he was dead, the pain he was in deserved multiple mercy bullets. After a few seconds of trembling and blood oozing, he was silent, a ravaged body of plant dissection.

I ran out of the house and vomited, then fainted in the sunlight. I woke up again to Snowy licking my face in nervous swipes. I rolled over and looked at the sky and few trails of clouds.

"What is happening?" I said to myself through some tears.

Day 93

Yesterday, I burnt what was left of his body. I didn't want it to come back to life, again.

I'm not sure how to rationalize how or why they'd do something so horrible. I haven't been actively trying to understand their motives, it'd be ridiculous trying to decipher why they're killing, hunting, and stalking us, but occasionally a contemplative state drifts its way inside my hiding place.

Why are they doing this?

I can't possibly understand it. They mutilate, kill, and tear us apart, then rebuild us with straps of vine and flower to fulfill their ghastly illusions during the night. I'm not sure if Timothy was already dead before they tied him together like a bile-filled puppet. I hope he was dead when they did all those stitches to him. I wouldn't be surprised if Timothy had been alive, judging by their primal sadism in all their beastly matters. What's so sickening about the Unnamed is that they remember me. They look for trails, and impacts, and where I might be hiding.

They're not just mindless killers. I wish they were, but they aren't.

It was hard handling his little mutilated body. I covered it with a white sheet I found in their plant-fused linen closet. I had to chop the vines away to get it open. I covered his body in the sheet and threw him over my shoulder. I plugged my nose with toilet paper, and kept a pink towel on top of my shoulder, so his blood wouldn't leak out onto me. Who knows what bacteria are pooling about it, especially with all the Unnamed's influences on our ecology? His body, for how diced and ravaged it looked, was still heavy and awkward to carry. Snowy wouldn't come towards the house while I retrieved him.

She knew something was off all along. I'm a little demoralized by how perceptive the animals are, and how I keep falling into these traps. The monsters don't threaten animals, yet, dogs have an incredible amount of intuition about the Unnamed.

I burnt his body outside the doorway with some gasoline from a red can my father had left around, and a long lighter I used for barbecues. I couldn't be around the smell, so I immediately ran away from the blaze. I was so disgusted by everything—I forgot to say something special for the little boy's funeral. I'm low on material anyways. I did grab a family photo out of the house on top of a white mantel above the fireplace. The picture was of his father and mother. They were holding him over a teal-water pool at some hotel. They were smiling, happy, and full of bright eyes.

The picture was evaporated by the flames in seconds. The body took much longer.

I didn't stay there for all of it. I couldn't watch his mutilated form sizzle away between uneven flames.

Last night, I stayed silent and motionless in the darkness. I couldn't get Timothy's face out of my mind. The sealed skin, the mumbling, the alive but rotting flesh, it'll never go away. It was yet another reason to never move in the darkness, to barely breathe. The drum sounded like normal, and between each faraway boom I waited for the thud of reanimated flesh to sound against the van's hollow sides. There was nothing but the drums, and few illusions sizzling across the gloom in false light. It was quiet and calm, like the drumming world wanted me to sit with what I'd witnessed.

Today, Snowy and I stayed away from the house for the most part. I actually stopped by to make sure his ashes weren't disturbed. I put the final parts in a small hole in his backyard. There were toys beaming through the heavy plants, and a swing set with dangling ivy. It looked like a happy place, so I think he'd be okay being buried there. I wish we could get buried whole, but the Unnamed desecrate us so easily.

After our burial today, and to make sure everything wasn't disturbed at the old phantom house, Snowy and I went swimming again. We stayed out in the water as long as we could. I counted clouds, and skipped stones across the clear water. Nothing moved in the overgrown world. I needed the tranquility, serenity, and everything else associated with those two words. There are so many nightmares now. I'm not sure where to even start.

I fed Snowy a few extra treats. I hope she likes them. I hope she's happy.

FRANCIS

Day 94

Last night, the strangest thing happened in the sky. There were planes. I'm not sure how many. I couldn't get a good glimpse through the window of the smashed and tilted van. I squeezed my body close to the window facing the garage, and its prickly crumbles of mortar. I didn't want to gawk through the other windows, just in case the Unnamed noticed me and came tearing through this thin-metal shell. I can't stand hiding in these flimsy spots. One of the big Unnamed could shred it in one swing of its obscene claw.

The most obvious spots are the safest though, the Unnamed completely overlook them. Their negligence is the only source of survival for us now. Not that there is "us." Who knows how many people are left with this parade of horrors.

I'm guessing it's not many, but I'm hoping to be surprised.

The planes hit shortly after midnight, while the drum was thundering in full force to its abomination-summoning rhythm.

Where do they come from? Why are they here? I hate these nagging questions. I feel like whoever finds these diary entries will think I've been whining this entire time. That I've been musing over the same plants, dreams, and monsters this entire time. The repetition of it all, the drum, the plants, it's like I notice nothing else. It's hard not to notice anything else.

At first, there were just jet roars between the drums, drowning out the solitary boom of some faraway devil. Then, the engines disappeared in hydraulic-charged cries, like when old jetliners would finally roar away across the sky after a casual droll.

I wonder if I'll ever ride on a plane again.

In the beginning, I didn't even pay attention to their rocket-sharp trails in the deep. Then, they returned in peppering bursts of what I could assume was machine gun fire. Bursts filled the air around the van, and sprinkles of random debris fell against it in hollow clicks and clacks. None of the explosions were close enough to drop anything on me of any substance. After a few rattling claps of rubble, the air was heavy with a dusty and brackish hue. The moonlight made it look like a thick and chalky fog had fallen across the neighborhood. The heat made it sink onto Snowy and I like a pet cloud from some old cartoon.

I was happy to hear the planes battling with the unknown and Unnamed darkness circling the skies at night. In fact, the way it sounded with their concise bullet fire and dipping engines, the battle was a planned operation. All the other scenarios where planes have tried to fly during the drum have ended in obscene failure.

The few glimpses I got of the actual combat from my mired spot were strange, but slightly invigorating. The planes were wide, sharp, and legendary looking. I loved jets when I was kid, and F-14's were pretty common back then. These looked just like those, only they looked newer and painted black. They'd fire long strings of bullets, which glowed like streaks of sharp fireflies. They must be tracers to determine where the bullets should hit. I'm not sure they do any good.

The night sky looks alive, like it's writhing, like a dark cloak being thrown against a rumpled fire. Shadows chase the planes like flowing lost birds with white faces and claws. I wish I wasn't so far away so I could see their details. I want to see their faces. I need to see their faces. I need them to show themselves. Not just the Unnamed ruling the air, but these others.

Only glimpses, I've only gotten glimpses.

Every time the jets would unleash a narrow cloud of gunfire on these living shards of darkness, the same bullets would fly back at them in nearly identical salvos. It was almost like they were firing and fighting into reflections of the night sky. The majority of these bounce-back shots would shred the jets into fiery scraps of plummeting metal. Others would dodge and fly higher into the backwards deep, with monsters in their wake. Sometimes, planes would work in pairs, and when one plane would engage one of the Flying Unnamed, and the other would fire when the beast would pause to mimic the bullets, and fire at its small white point of a face. A few of the monsters disappeared from this coordinate attack, and popped in the air like chained fire and drew up into themselves like some sort of shadowy whirlpool.

Before it really had started, the battle was over, and I listened to the sounds of falling debris for the rest of the night.

I couldn't tell who was winning, until I woke up in the morning and walked around the neighborhood.

At least seven planes had crashed like broken bugs into crumpled houses and bent streetlights. None of them smoked, flamed, or showed any sign of the previous drum's battle. The Unnamed must've put them out. They hate fire, just like any plant-warped monster would. The plants completely enveloped their strewn metal carcasses, like the pilots didn't even have a chance before they wrapped around them. The cockpits to each plane were smashed apart like a leveled clear egg. Blood dried along their edges. They didn't even have a chance to eject during their dogfight.

A few roofs collapsed while I was walking around today. They echoed against the green neighborhood. All that was left of last night's firefight were a few ghostly echoes, and some vanishing rubble.

Day 95

It happened again last night. Something came sliding down the rocks and stubborn plants. I could hear the form flatten the spiny stalks along the ground as it moved. It was a corpse, just like Timothy. It wasn't just the sound either, but the feeling, the hopelessness of being reanimated out of some evisceration from the monsters. The pain of being torn apart by their hidden claws, and sewed back together in hasty vine-laced stitches with blood oozing out the lippy sides -- it must've been unbearable.

The sound came around two in the morning, just like the last one. I've been waiting for it to come again, listening for that dragging of unwanted meat to slam against the van. I waited for it between every hollow beat of the drum. I knew it would come for some reason. I knew Timothy couldn't have been the only one they did this to.

What sewed them back together? Are the Unnamed really that good at human needle-point? What is doing this? Who is bringing them back to life, making them phantoms, and letting them die again? Is it these Builders?

I hate writing down questions. It makes me seem whiny.

The weighted sound of its hand beating against the empty side of the van lasted for just a few minutes. I don't even know how it managed that it. It looked like Timothy could barely breathe in that sewn up state. There was gasping in the darkness too, as it scratched for help. I wanted to help it. I wanted to let whoever it was inside, so I could end their pain with a few silenced bullets. I couldn't open the door though; it just wasn't possible. They could've been watching. A limbless corpse pulling itself along in the midst of the drum, it's hard not to think it wouldn't be noticeable.

I wanted to whisper to it through the walls. What would I say though? What would I say?

Eventually, the sound drifted away, and the dark sudden slams of the drum were the only echo piercing the night. I stayed up all night with my back against the blue upholstery, and with Snowy sleeping beneath my propped up legs. She didn't whine or cry when the dragging came around. I wonder what that means? It must mean something.

In the morning, I looked for more signs of whatever tried to get my attention last night. I know it had to be another one of those things that Timothy was turned into. If the Unnamed needed the whole night to be swimming with these things, then I'm sure there were other patched together bodies. There would have to be hundreds of them hidden around these plants and wrapped over homes. The thought of them moaning to themselves in the darkness, waiting to be killed like Timothy was; it's unsettling, and makes me not want to move.

I walked around the neighborhood, checking for signs that someone could've been moving last night. It was impossible to tell. The plants have rolled over everything. Now only green remains. It glows with a stern and commanding radiance. As I walked around, roofs collapsed in crumbling crashes of wooden clatter. Crows caw upwards in black spirals from the shattering sound, but then resettle on another pile of disheveled debris. *The world is becoming flat, and in a year or two, we'll have nothing to hide in at night. I can't be too worried about what happens that far down the road.*

I walked to Rainbow Foods and the lake again. I took a different route, around the hospital, just to be safe. We played in the water, and rolled around on the grass outside the shore. The water keeps things tranquil and quiet. It's like sitting next to a non-angry ocean. We stayed there all day. I can't concern myself too much with finding whatever was outside my van last night. I'll have to start scrounging for supplies soon, and then I'll search for more clues, and determine if what happened to Timothy wasn't an isolated phenomenon.

Around four in the afternoon, we left the lake and walked back towards my house. We were going to walk by Timothy's too. I wanted to make sure nothing funny was going on. We passed the parking lot outside Rainbow Foods, and the wind picked up a bit, throwing dark blue and red petals everywhere. On the marquee, where I sprayed that warning about Timothy a week ago, a new message was scribbled on the marquee in sky blue paint.

It said, "Watch out for Francis."

My skin pulled tight with nervousness, as I played over the sentence again, and again, and again in my mind. There was more than one? I was right about last night. Even worse, it was an illusion in the daylight that might try and trick me. I looked around frantically at the empty roads, the plant-eaten buildings, the quiet broken down cars, and the trembling sheets of ivy. It could be anywhere? It could find my hiding spot, and lead them to me in the day or night. That one that came through the daylight to kill me, I'm sure they'll be more.

I might have to start hiding in multiple spots, to keep them guessing.

After a few panting stares at empty alleys, I realized I wasn't ever going to know what was coming next. My dog might. She was wise. I need to listen to her reactions.

On our walk back to the van, we walked by Timothy's house. I stopped outside of it and went to one knee. I aimed my M16 at it, and breathed deeply between tears and uncontrollable bowels.

The house was clean again. The plants had gone away. Someone was sitting on the stoop.

Day 96

I couldn't approach him.

Whoever it was, whatever it was, I just didn't want to know. If it was Timothy, if he'd come back to life and bloomed out of the ground like a twisted-corpse sewn flower. I wouldn't know what to do. I wouldn't know to kill him again, attack his spore copy, or burn his house to the ground. I'm thinking that final action will be the one. Burn it, raze it, and let it turn to a smoldering layer of uneven vinyl and broken wood.

I need to do something. I can't just let this other world have free reign here, sending monsters to and fro, and resurrecting a pulpy mass of carved meat whenever they want. It's insane, everything about it is, and even the sunlight crawling down between the steaming plants has a hint of madness to it. I don't know why, or how, but that dusty yellow light doesn't feel the same anymore. It's almost like we've been betrayed. The earth has broiled into a jungle of monsters and dead men, who twist into different shapes like a spiked cloud of smoke.

I watched the figure on the stoop for a while. It was a man, a tall one, with his head in his hands. I couldn't tell if he was crying or shuttering with his posture. I know he was bent over into his legs, like someone who is stretching out for some sort of sporting event. It looked unnatural, like maybe his back was broken or unhinged. I almost thought about peppering that haunted doorway with a ring of bullets, but I remembered what happened in my first confrontation with Timothy. They're made out of some golden pollen, a living cloud of sorts. My bullets wouldn't do anything. Still, it would be satisfying to shoot them.

I looped around the haunted house. I avoided all the empty spots between the crumbled buildings, just in case the man randomly turned around and noticed me. I'm not sure what he could be, he could be normal, but it doesn't really matter.

Everything appears to be hunting us.

Last night didn't really help diminish this dark reality.

Yesterday, after avoiding the monster portal, Snowy and I hid in the van before the drum even started. When it finally started its demon-thunder around eight, I was almost happy that the night was getting started. Hiding extra-long is tough, simply because I'm always hiding in some way, and it gets hard on the psyche. You feel like such a failure, a coward, and everything laughs at you up from the flowers to the vines. If the Unnamed are capable of laughing, I know they must be somewhere deep in the shadows.

I slept for the first half of the night. These last few days have been exhausting, and even the seemingly infinite fear from those sewn up bodies has a limit. I was so exhausted I didn't dream, which was a sweaty blessing curled against the sideways passenger seat of my van.

Around two in the morning, I woke up to a strange sound. There was a snorting sound outside the van and garage. It was low, sharp, and slightly animal-like in its throaty clicks. It sounded like there was a voice mixed into it, a man's voice to be exact. I could hear the voice answer, like it was trying to stop the growling. There was a carving sound above the van, right below where my shed use to be. They were long crumbly carves, which popped up strips of hidden rock and hardened soil. There were more grumbles, and something was smashed behind the van, like a wall or something. After the deep rips and bashes, there was a silence between the drum and night. Then something crumbled down next to the van. It was the garage wall. A few bricks broke through the upside windshield in the front of the vehicle.

I kept quiet, even though I wanted to scream. Snowy was shivering between my feet. She pressed her snout up against my leg, like that little gesture could keep everything away. Moonlight spilled in the broken window in some jagged shapes. It looked pretty for a second, then the snarling continued, followed by incoherent mumbles.

I stayed pressed up against the opposite side of the van, away from the tempered horror outside. How could anything be moving out there? The Unnamed would rip them to bits, and reanimate them, how could anything move? They had to be in league with them, a part of their collective. Only, whatever this goddamn thing was, it had a different method of looking. It wasn't going to hide or stalk, but rumble around looking for a confrontation.

It sounded like an animal, and because it does, it makes me think it's mortal. It's a weird sensation holding my gun. I want to kill it. The trigger feels so light and arid. It just sounds like something that can be killed.

I didn't move all night. The sound left eventually, but not till a few more pieces of rock were slashed and gutted. I've become an expert in keeping my breath the only moving force in the humid darkness.

In the morning, I explored the area of growling. The plants had been slashed apart where they covered the ground like a sea of green string. They hadn't grown back together? The pavement had been torn upwards, like the concrete ground was nothing but soft soil. The slashes were a foot deep at least, and dew had collected inside of them in silver droplets. Brick walls, which had been extra fortified by the plants, lay in piles of cluttered rock and dust.

Something strong had been here last night. Something new and wicked. The Unnamed didn't bother it, so it must've been terrifying. I only walked a hundred feet away from the van, when the wind picked up and the sun felt heavier. The dew was making rising fogs against across the green world, and a blue sky sat unchallenged above.

"You need to move," a voice said behind. The voice was deep and sharp.

It sounded eerily familiar.

At first I didn't move. I wanted to run away. It's the typical first reaction in this lost and plant-etched world. Run first, theorize later. I'd ask questions later, but there is no one real around to talk to or ask. The natural world doesn't help with this fear and flight reaction. Whenever the air moves upwards and the wind bends with it, my knees shift awkwardly and I just want to run in whatever direction I'm able.

"Don't run," the deep voice said soothingly. There was a throaty tremble at the end of the statement, like something was trying to stop it from speaking. Snowy was glued to my foot trembling, with one tiny brown paw sitting in the air like a bird's neck.

"If you run, something inside this body will trigger. Then, I'll chase you, and I'll kill."

I wanted to run. There are two grenades strapped to my vest below my right shoulder. The one little movement it would take to grab these weapons seemed like a long lost distance.

"I'm not like the others, not like the little boy. You'd better not run," the voice said. I dropped the narrow nozzle of the M16 down to my waist. I wanted my gun there to turn around with me. I needed it there to have a level shot at this talking monster. The backyard slopes downward, it would at least give me an accurate line of fire. The sunlight tugged at my eyes as I turned around. Grasshoppers bumbled about the air like temporary paper missiles.

"You just told me to move. Now you're telling me not to run?" I said.

"If you run, you'll provoke him, and I can't say I'll be responsible for what happens next," the voice said.

"If you're going to kill me, can you at least take care of my dog?" I said.

"I'm trying to avoid the killing part, now, just turn around. You know we don't care about dogs," he said.

The backyard of my house looked wild and untamed, in every measure of the two words. The downed tree was entangled into the earth like a veined fog. The shed was gone, the roof of my house was sinking further and further into the earth. I'm not sure what it was. Maybe it was the utter panic running through me, but at that exact moment, I noticed how foreign everything looked. My old home looked out of place against the building jungle.

"Okay, I'm turning around. You want me to put my weapon away?"

"Leave it out. For god's sake hurry up. It won't do any good anyways," he said.

I turned around quickly, with the gun pressed up into my shoulder and my finger playing soft on the trigger. Behind me a man stood leaning against the sideways van. He was tall, whitish, with thinning brown hair and a narrow face. He was wearing blue jeans, with a white t-shirt with specs of blood dried all over it in odd twirls and shapes. His skin looked unusually pink, like it had been painted over by a dried brush in heavy streaks. I wanted to stare at the skin, but his eyes had my complete attention. They were bright green, like a whole sheet of the world around us had been boiled down into two round gems. There were no whites, no irises, or corneas.

He was clearly some sort of monster. He was clearly some sort of Unnamed.

"Yes," he said, while I gawked at him

"Yes what?" I said trying to close my mouth.

"I'm one of them. Like Timothy, only he couldn't turn at night. They tried to make it work with the sewing and all, but it really didn't stick," he said flatly.

"Who? What sent you out in the daylight?" I asked with a shaking gun.

"I can't talk about it, or I'll have a hard time containing," he said putting his head in his hands.

"What? Contain what?"

"I'm two things in one. During the day, like Timothy, I'm just another fake person walking around. At night, I'm a thing. You saw my warning right? They call me Francis, and I'm not even sure why. I know that wasn't my name before. I'm on borrowed parts."

"Parts?" I asked.

"You've seen what they've done, it's all parts, so don't be stupid," he said pulling his head back with a grin. Flowers were hanging from where his teeth would be. The gums looked white and dead. I started to walk away from him slowly, keeping the building at my back.

"You have to move. I almost had you last night. I saw you come out this morning, so my other will know tonight. You'll have to hide anew, someplace different and interesting," he said kicking the van.

"It was you carving up the place?" I said trembling.

"Not me directly, but close enough, apparently," he said, pointing at his chest.

"I don't understand."

"Timothy instructed you in how to speak to us. I heard him say it."

I reached my limit.

"Yeah? Well, I'm sorry, but I don't trust monsters and walking corpses that goddamn often. When the drum starts you go crazy huh? You know, I've killed a fair amount of your makers, Builders, dads, whatever they are. I've killed them." I said.

I shook my gun slightly and spat him.

"They know," he said walking away. He was moving fast, like he was afraid someone else might've been listing.

"Where are you going?" I yelled.

"Just make sure to hide in a different spot, boy. It'll be good for you," he said. In a few moments he vanished like a thin white line into the tangled underbrush behind the garage. I wanted to chase him down. I wanted to beat the answer out of him somehow. Maybe I could light him on fire? That reminds me, I need to burn that house to the ground. I don't care what happens to it.

I waited a few minutes to see if he would return. I don't know why, but I sort of wanted him to. I wanted to speak to him, no matter if he was some dark extension of that haunted house down the block. I believed him about leaving my hiding spot. He clearly saw it. He would lead them my way in the night, and it'd be the end of me in one quick flurry of wild claws.

I grabbed the rest of my supplies out of my linen closet, and put them in my black duffel bag. I'd typically take it with me on vacations. It'd been to both Florida and San Francisco. It was weird using it for something else, like the luggage felt confused or betrayed. I'm becoming more and more paranoid. I know it's warranted, but should I keep worrying about ordinary objects from the old world?

I worry about them, and I don't know why?

I carried the duffel bag with me as I walked around. I made sure the gangly man with the fake skin wasn't watching. Tomorrow, I'll burn that house to the ground. It should go up easily, especially with all the green kindling attached to the earth around it. I'll use all the gasoline I have to get it to burn.

I found a half smashed open car about three blocks away from my house. It was a Jeep Cherokee I think, but I can't really be sure with all the plants all over it. Inside, I set up all my stuff in the passenger seats. I scrapped away enough of the vines and flowers to curl down beneath the seats. It's in the open, between a four-way intersection and some streetlights. It shouldn't be suspicious to them, especially not this Francis guy. I wonder what he is. The Builders sent another one after me? How many times can they try and kill me?

I stayed inside the car the rest of the day. I didn't want to move. I don't want to move. The drum will start soon. I wonder what it'll bring.

Day 97

Last night, whatever Francis was or wasn't, something different came out into the darkness. He didn't find me, but I heard him trying. At first, shortly after seven, the drum started in those distant booms half a green hell away. I stayed in the backseat of the Jeep with a blanket to throw over us. Snowy slept next to my feet. She was very still, like she knew about the fear associated with this new monster.

I, however, wanted to scream the entire night.

I couldn't throw the blanket over us permanently, it was already too hot inside the car, and with the blanket we'd practically suffocate. If the Unnamed or Francis came toward us, I'd throw it over us in one last ditch effort to hide. I really didn't want to do it; especially, with Snowy already panting in her sleep from the excessive heat. When the sun set and those pollen-thick orange beams bled through the broken glass of the car, I bet it was close to ninety degrees inside. I poured a little water over my face, and a little on Snowy's sleeping body, which she wasn't happy about and let out a mild groan.

I rubbed her belly until she fell asleep, again.

The night started quiet. Nothing bustled about the waning blooms of sun or twilight. No shadows crept over the car, and nothing scraped up against it. I wonder if they knew I was inside the van early on. I remember hearing their claws scrapping in long and torturous scratches. Maybe it was them testing the area, seeing if they could provoke me out of this hiding spot.

They've got some system setup, or some sort of hive mind. The Builders must be their commanders, kings, or queens. Thank god for all those science fiction movies to make my deductive reasoning about this unknown situation more reasonable. I never thought they'd prepare me for anything, except a large amount of nostalgia upon watching them on Netflix when it was still around.

I miss movies.

I actually slept for the first five hours of the drum, despite the new threat from the random illusion-man named Francis. I've learned not to distract myself about why something is the way it is, in this new green land. That thought process sets you back the moment it starts. It'll distract you and fester like when a woman shoots you down for no apparent reason. I shouldn't have put that, my thoughts are drifting back to Ling.

I can't think about her. I won't. I want to, but I won't. It hurts from the bottoms of my feet up into my ears. This weird numbing pain, like my skin doesn't want to react to the rest of my body.

Stop it.

At quarter after three, he came looking for me. The illusions were partially going in the intersection where I was hiding. There were no false portraits, pictures, or images dancing about the darkness in hollow clouds. Only the streetlights turned on in fake amber beams. The dust and pollen from the vine wrapped world hung in the air below each ray, like it wants to stay constantly shifting in a menacing fog.

At first, there were a variety of growls along the street, both low and high, like they were trying to figure out how to communicate with another. Smashes of broken rock and screaming metal would thunder between the guttural two-sided conversations. Next, trees were uprooted in crackled wrenches, and the soil beneath their networks popped upward in disheveled gasps.

"No, no trees you fool," I heard a voice say in the background. Some dark murmurs echoed back like a barking dog.

Eventually, the living-train drifted by the car and stormed down the pavement. It stopped when close to me and let out a sharp snort. The Unnamed clearly didn't have a sense of smell. If they did, I would've been killed a long time ago. Snowy woke up when it came close to us. She looked at me as it staggered around the car in labored steps.

I wanted to whisper it was okay. I wanted to tell her not to be scared.

Only the old world allowed me to lie so much.

The ground swelled to its steps. The car creaked against each grunting dash, which was erratic and frenzied. It had centered my location, but couldn't actually find me.

"The car, check the car," it grunted darkly.

"No, not out here, he's too smart," someone whined.

"We know he's near, check it, check something-" it gurgled.

"No, no, he's back at the house, get him there," the other interrupted.

"Yes, yes, he could just have things here. Things that have been on his body," the dark one said.

The earth bounced up and down. The frame of the plant-slashed Jeep clanked outwards between each boom. The Unnamed barely brushed against the plants when they moved. They were the definition of a sharp wind.

I wanted to watch it as the growling drifted away. I couldn't risk moving though. Maybe it was better that I didn't get to see this new walking nightmare.

In the morning, I peeked out of the broken windows at the fog-pillowed land of glowing plants and pollen. Nothing was watching. Not a goddamn thing. We started to walk back towards my house three blocks away. The pavement had been creased by its feet. The plants had filled in the dips in just one night.

"Nice job last night," a voice said behind me.

Francis was there on my right. He was standing on top of a wrapped-mountain of plants, which had swirled over a broken roof. Snowy didn't even sense him. He looked the same as yesterday, only he looked redder, like his skin trying to fall off.

"You'd better hide again though, you're lucky we argued about it," he said with a close-lipped smile.

"What? What do you mean?" I staggered out.

"Hide, keep it going, you need to stay away," he said again.

"What is happening? Why can't you say anything more?" I screamed, shaking my gun at him.

Francis fell to the ground shaking his body back and forth.
A third arm popped out of his right shoulder, like a sharp string of
lime-green twine. A golden blade was attached to it. I've
known them before. He shrugged his shoulder backwards to hide
the flapping appendage like he was embarrassed.

"Run!" He screamed with an uneven voice.

I didn't move.

"Run!" he screamed again. "He's coming."

At first I didn't move. I'm tired of being so predictable, but
the moment his skin started to part and whatever was inside of him
broiled outwards, I couldn't goddamn move. The moment that
bladed arm broke free of the fake flesh, something inside of me went
numb and weak. I felt it deep into my ribcage. I think it was hope
escaping. Francis started swinging around against himself, like he
was being unraveled by some invisible hands. The tempest of plants
beneath his shaking knees pulsated outwards, like they were synced
with his heartbeat. I vomited as I watched it.

I hate barfing all the time. I'm so weak. I hope there are
others who are stronger than me. Are there any others?

"Run you bitch, get outta here!" Francis waved with a
bloody forearm. Snowy started barking. It snapped me back to
reality. How many times does this have to happen to me?

"He'll kill you, now run," he mumbled again. He curled
over himself, and his back started to splint with peaking vines.

More hot wind and rushing trees, it's always the same thing.
The world shakes to them and their abominations.

"Run, now run, go away and hide," he screamed again with gargled vibrations.

I wanted to doubt him and his thrashing body. There was no drum, no random storm to signify the Unnamed's presence. I fired my M16 at him. The bullets sounded like metallic pepper in the air. I've fired my gun so many times before, but this time the sound seemed to sting my chest. The bullets plopped into his body in bile-long strings. Green vines wrapped through the freshly punctured wounds, and his form started to glow with this leeching yellow light. His skin swelled up like it needed air. It grew, and it grew.

"Run you bitch, run!" He screamed as his voice turned hollow and empty. Snowy and I sprinted away. She ran fluidly, like a little brown raindrop over the jungle floor. I tripped and stumbled over the vines. A few times, I even almost fell. It would've been all over if I did. I know it. The world ahead of us seemed to be moving, but staying still at the same time: the overly crowded trees hanging onto the roads, the crushed in roofs of houses with their layers of leaves and speckled vines, the long pools of bold flowers, broken cars, and piles of wood shuddering like they wanted to distract me. I heard snarling behind me, and some sort of splitting sound was bleeding into the wind.

He was changing. I felt bad. I didn't even know him. Why is this happening? Did they make Timothy like this too?

I dashed to my right between two wrapped houses, and dived beneath a deck between the buildings. The wood was paneled in thin crisscross streaks, and there was a bunch of charcoal packages underneath it. I pulled the bags around us and curled up against the wall. The ground started to tremble again, and that snorting sound cut the air. Dust fell on top of us from the shattered deck. I replaced the magazine on my gun. The clanking and snapping sound seemed too loud. The air was so quiet besides the growling. Why is it never quiet around me? Why must it always move?

Something started to walk past the house. At first, I could only see its shadow hulking and dragging along, like a bloated mass of sharp muscle. The air turned heavy with it. Snowy stayed perfectly still beneath my legs. I could only see a little bit from over the crumpled bags. The shadow sat over us sniffing. There wasn't any dialogue this time, no arguing back and forth. Only breathing and grunting, which the Unnamed never did. It's part of them, but it's completely different.

I sort of missed the old Unnamed.

After about ten minutes, the shadow slowly stumbled away. I didn't move. I couldn't. We sat there for two hours with barely a breath moving between us. Sweat dripped off my face and onto Snowy. We waited until we couldn't breathe anymore. I walked out into the opening between the two houses. Nothing moved. The wind stayed quiet and non-intrusive. Snowy followed me. Her posture seemed normal and her tail was bubbly. I knew we were temporarily safe.

We ran back towards my house. I had dropped the duffel bag of supplies where I'd been earlier with Francis. I ran as quietly as possible, so I could hear his vibrations if he was coming. We weren't far down the block when I noticed the untouched black duffel bag sitting like a lone vinyl star in the middle of the green road. We dashed sideways as we approached it, and hid against a car that had been thrown through the front door of a house across the street. Plants hung off it in a brambly curtain. It was from this angle and hiding spot that I noticed it.

My house was gone.

It was completely pulverized into a shattered wreck of broken wood, cracked mortar, and layered plants. I tried to keep calm, to keep my heart from sinking into my feet and making me faint. It was flattened. Francis had done this, he remembered where I lived. My home was gone, completely and utterly, like it never existed in this green world. They had nearly taken everything me, but this was my sanctuary, a place to hide from the monsters and remember the old world.

I started to cry.

I cried so hard I couldn't breathe. Snowy kept putting her snout under my arm as I shivered. I eventually pulled her tight and watched the wind pushing the overburdened eaves. Snowy kept pushing me, and I kept crying.

"I know," I said wiping my face with the grimy back of my hand. "I know we have to hide soon."

Day 98

Last night, we hid in an abandoned house two blocks away from our previous night's hiding spot. It was big, sturdy, and plated with grey bricks at its base. Plants had eaten the majority of the foundation, siding, and roof, but the whole structure looked like it could last a few more months. I'm getting worried about structures and their foundations as the plants worm across them in their green sheets. It's all so heavy, the entire world looks weighed down like wet clothes. Even the shadows drool that way in long and dangling masses.

We didn't have much time to scour for a good spot before the drums started. I couldn't go back to the broken down car in the middle of the intersection. Francis was nearby when I crawled out of it. He could've told them where I was, or where I came from. I wonder how he talks to them. I wonder how they know his thoughts. It's all a big mystery, which has gotten deeper and thicker with the plants each morning. It's almost like my fear feeds them, and they bristle their green waves higher with each new nightmare.

Things are watching me in the shadows. I know they are there. Whatever Francis turned in to, he was sent here to hunt in the daylight and to live without the drum. I can't trust the daylight anymore either.

The house Snowy and I stayed in was big, covered in hardwood floors, and coiled with soft and sharp layers of vines. There was broken glass everywhere. I had to carry Snowy inside under my arm. I checked the house for survivors, or signs of

300

occupation, but there wasn't anything. There were still some canned goods in the kitchen, so I filled my duffel bag with them. I'm getting low on food and water. I'll need to start scavenging soon, but I'm scared with Francis walking around. How does something that huge just disappear?

I still need to burn down Timothy's old house. I know it's a link for them. These other monsters didn't start appearing till the swimming darkness did.

Inside our hiding house was a metal staircase to the second floor of the house. I wouldn't walk up there though. I don't want to fall through the floor. Beneath the stairs, there was small door into a storage closet. There were no scraps on it, or signs of the Unnamed. Inside it, there was nothing, no coats or clothes. I wonder if the people that lived here took all their coats out before they fled. Why would they do that? I managed to get us inside the dark little chamber right before the drum started hammering away in the darkness. The shadows snapped around us in the fading sunlight popping through the broken windows. Inside the kitchen, a narrow window lined above the sink. I haven't watched that much sunlight right before the drum since it all started.

It made sad. I don't know why.

I closed the door and sat in the darkness with Snowy. My gun was ready, and leaning against the door. The heat made the blackness feel thick and swimming. I listened for them, but all I could hear was the dark air rattling broken wood and rubble. There were some scratching sounds too, but they didn't stick around very long. I fell asleep for a few hours, but some sounds woke me up around two in the morning. There were people talking outside the door. It was normal volume. They weren't trying to whisper like they were hiding from the Unnamed. Water was running, and I heard an oven door clank open and close. Light was bleeding in from the bottom of the door. Footsteps thumped against the floor. There was laughter. People were happy.

They couldn't have been real.

Snowy started to scratch at the door. Something must've been taunting her, since she never was interested in them before. I scooped her up and pressed her against me. The door clicked open slowly. I expected every ghoul, ghost, and phantom to be waiting there for us, and for them to literally be ushering in the Unnamed through the door. I was prepared to fire my gun into the shapes and lights. It would be a rapid death. The Unnamed would come in quick and fast. I'd be dead so quick. The door opened fully into the noisy kitchen. There was nothing, just the same darkness, debris, and plants. It looked even emptier than before. The sounds and lights had my hopes.

A shadow bled through the moonlight outside the front door. I pulled the closet shut and pressed up against the back wall. Something came inside the house.

I heard the scrapping sound that's always associated with the smaller Unnamed. It brushed up against the door, and I could hear its weight flexing against the wall. A roaring sound ripped open the night, and a crashing echoed through the sheet-rock. The

Unnamed left, I heard its blades scuttle away like a devilish crab. The roaring continued throughout the night. It mixed with the drum, which made the instrument seem tame and lifeless despite what it summoned. I slept from all the panic.

I woke up in the heat and rising steam. I staggered out into the empty house. I couldn't do anything but walk to the lake. I need to get water. I need to get away from all the horrors. On my way there, nothing moved, and if it did, I'd throw every bullet at it that I could. I don't care anymore. I'm so tired of hiding. We made it to the lake, and immediately started swimming. I didn't even take off all my clothes. Across the golden-blue water something moved and shook the trees. Something was watching and waiting for us.

Let it come.

Day 99

Last night, I hid inside the Rainbow foods with all the many empty shelves, cobwebs, vines, and broken boxes of rotted food. After that thing across the water saw me yesterday, Snowy and I went and retrieved our duffel bag from the house, since I had left it inside the closet. I didn't want to move it, and have something distract me. It's a weird worry.

I'm not sure what made the trees vibrate and clatter like a lost leafy seizure. They looked so unhinged against this hidden force. The plants have looked so permanent and plentiful, like nothing could shiver their roots or make them tremble. They have dominion. Complete and utter dominion. I hate them so much. Every little bud and flower, they can all be burned to ash to be spread like grounded jewels into the hot air. I hate them.

During the night, behind all the shelves inside Rainbow Foods, Snowy and I counted the trembling thunder of the drum. I'm trying to figure out if there is a pattern. Before, I wouldn't even bother. There were too many other things to worry about. Now though, the darkness has a sense of fear, like one of the Unnamed's own creations has run amuck, and driven the sharp abominations into hiding. The night before it was right outside the door, the Unnamed with its glittering and sharp extensions. Then, something snarled and roared, and the lifeless shadow fled away back into the depths. What could scare them away? It's no wonder the nights have become docile to their sliding forms.

Inside the Rainbow, we hid inside a bunch of white cluttered shelves with broken edges. It stunk like sour meat. The type of flesh you'd see at the bottom of a meat factory floor. It stinks. I hate it. The pocket of twisted metal we hid in kept the stench from surrounding us, but the flies still bunched around like sheets of crackling smog. At times, they were so loud in the metal darkness, it almost blocks out the drum. Almost being the key word. Nothing makes it go away. It'll always be there booming in the deep.

It rules. It's king.

In the gloom of Rainbow nothing moved besides those flies. The plants worming about the rubble whooshed against the wind blowing in from the desolate parking lot. A few streetlights powered up with their phantom lights. It makes me ill to see their glowing orange halos just outside the shattered automatic doors. A few more shines of light blipped nearby in red, green, and orange glows.

They made a stoplight work. That's impressive.

I fell asleep counting the shadows beneath their colored glows. In the morning, I pulled Snowy and I out of our cluttered mass of old shelving and broken boxes. I was pulling her out of the rubble when a shadow drifted through the shattered doors. It was massive. It blocked out the sun and made the whole store cold.

I grabbed Snowy and we ran towards the back exit.

Something crashed behind us, and the store shook inwards like toy logs. Ceiling panels collapsed around us, and a few shards of their plastic skin caught my face as I ran. The taste of blood can really wake you up in the morning. We made it to the exit door and smashed through it into the sun. I was blinded for a second and tripped throwing Snowy to the ground. She yelped and rolled, but got to her feet and ran for a dumpster down the back lot of the grocery store. I followed without much hesitation. The Unnamed don't scare her really, but this thing most certainly did. The dumpster was a dark blue box with plants wrenched across it. There would be no way to get inside of it before that thing came through the brick wall or door. We crawled underneath it.

I kept the M16 pointed down the pavement at the base of the exit door.

The crashing grew louder as I watched the green-encrusted wall of the building. In one loud pop the exit door flew off like a piece of tinfoil, and clattered down the pavement in sparking streaks. I held my breath and aimed the gun. This was it. What could it be? I needed to see it.

A single hand wrapped around the doorway. It was a reddish-green, with spikes of gold bone and black veins. The same shade as the spores that hide the Unnamed in the shadows. The hand was huge, at least the size of my torso, even before I lost all this weight from my steady diet of canned food. When it gripped the doorway, the walls crackled to it, like it could tear it all down if it wanted. I kept the gun level. I was shaking, but I had to aim it.

The hand pulled away into the faraway square slowly. It was thinking about something. A few narrow clouds of brick-heavy dust fell off the roof and played a pattern in the hot wind. Nothing moved, the hand never reappeared and ground never trembled.

How could it know? I was ready to barrage it with bullets. If it was Francis, it would have some human intelligence, which meant it might be hunting me with some sort of tact or method. I waited a few hours before running home. I wanted to be safe. When I got home, I forgot that it had been destroyed completely and utterly. I stared at it for a few hours with Snowy next to my leg. I didn't even hide. She eventually started to whine at me.

She knew we had to hide.

Day 100

Last night, they were out again in full force, scouring about the shadows in their demon-sharp trails. I wanted to kill them. I wanted to slowly open the door of this stranger's closet, and pepper the swirling emptiness with bullets until they tracked me down and tore me to shreds. I wanted this. I want more and more as each day goes by. It can't be though; they'd kill me in a second, in one quick swarm of golden blades and pulsating arms.

I haven't seen one of the big Unnamed for a while, the one with the enormous right arm, which can tear tanks apart like green clay. They must manage the smaller ones, a type of underling system with grunts and servants. I wish they were that short-sighted. I wish they had these elements of humanity to them. Then I know they could be tricked and defeated though pure tenacity and strategy.

Last night, I hid in the same closet as before, the one with all the illusions. I thought about finding a new place to hide, especially after that thing hunted me in Rainbow Foods. A daylight monster, that's just great. It's been only a little over a week since the Unnamed sent one of their foot-soldiers out of glooming portal down the block. Only one try at me beneath the sun, and I managed to kill it with just my bare hands and a hatchet. Direct hits don't kill them, even with a gun or grenade. Multiple hits, which jitter apart their cells from concussions, seem to do the trick. Only if you can hit them though, if you can, they move so fast and they blend in night to perfection.

The shadows might as well be hunting you against the drum. Maybe that's why they stretch and shutter when that grizzly instrument starts. The Unnamed frighten the shadows. I'm angrier than normal because yesterday after I came back to my house from hiding, not only had I forgotten it was destroyed, but knowing they came after my home to demoralize me was physically sickening.

They destroyed everything inside of it: the walls were ripped to pieces, the wood torn upwards in chunks, the furniture that hadn't been choked by the plants was pulverized, my appliances had disappeared completely, and my books were shredded. Something specific did it, something with a vendetta against me. They've had this rage before, the Unnamed. I've been a victim of it. This new monster, the thing that was Francis, is something different entirely. I'm sure I'll see it one of these days or nights. I'm sure it'll be a personal interaction.

Besides the drum and the reestablished shadows, the night passed without incident and illusions. I heard them on the other side of the closet door looking for me. They scraped as silently as they could, like a rat inside a jar with smoke. They couldn't get me though. I'll start to set traps for them again once this Francis thing is taken care of. I want it be gone.

In the morning, I took my time leaving my hiding spot and taking us out into the neighborhood. Clearly, there is something stalking us, but it's having a hard time actually isolating our location. We moved slowly between each broken and green-washed structure. We'd sit for a few minutes at each, and monitor the shattered buildings with their cluttered shadows.

This thing had such a shadow, it made the whole store cold yesterday.

I should see it coming, but I can't take any chances. We need to start scavenging for food and water again; the duffel bag keeps getting lighter. I don't want it all to sneak up on us. I'll procrastinate one more day on it. I can't think about anything but that shape in the sun yesterday.

We traveled in a big loop through the green and quiet neighborhood. Nothing moved, nothing shook the trees besides the wind. There were no lost horrors booming in the ground beneath the footsteps of some unchained behemoth.

It was quiet, serene, and overflowing with greenery. I'm not going to move anymore today. I'm not going to try and fight anything tonight.

It's been a hundred days now.

The world is a jade shadow of what it used to be. We always thought it'd be fun to rule the apocalyptic world, to dodge beasts and devils like in the movies with Charlton Heston or Will Smith.

Now, faces have been cut off. Bodies have been sewn together like miscellaneous slabs of meat. Illusions rule the darkness in spore-wild clouds.

Now, survival is as abstract as these monsters.

Now there are only the monsters, and me.

Made in the USA
Middletown, DE
10 February 2015